Dog-Gone Christmas

By Melinda Curtis

Acknowledgments

To my family, who love and support me in all I do.
To my team, who keep me sane.
And to Remington, a real life St. Bernard/Great Pyreneese
mix who is quite the talker.

Praise and Awards

Chapter One

"The abominable snowman is in our backyard!"

Marnie Haywood kept stirring the gravy. She had a few days to perfect her gravy-making technique before Christmas. She wasn't going to burn the gravy this year, especially since her in-laws were coming for the holiday.

Besides, the likelihood that a live snowman was in their sunny San Diego backyard was small.

Five year-old Alex jumped up and down next to her. "Abominable! Snowman!" He made claws with both hands and dropped his voice to a monster snarl. *"A-bom-in-a-ble! Snow-man!"*

Maybe it'd been a mistake to allow Alex to binge-watch Rudolph the Red Nose Reindeer and sample the baked goods she'd made to share with their friends and neighbors. He was supercharged, bursting with enough energy to power Rudolph's nose through a foggy all-nighter.

No fictional snowman was ruining Marnie's gravy. She stirred as vigorously as her son jumped.

And then they both stopped, because something growled. Something in their backyard.

Alex gripped her jean-clad leg. "I told you." He pointed to the glass slider behind her. The one leading to their condo's backyard.

A thin sheet of glass separated them from a huge white dog. A pony-sized dog. A slobber-on-the-slider, paws-as-big-as-softballs, jaws-as-big-as-bear-traps dog.

Marnie's insides shimmied like tinsel near a heating vent. This situation wasn't covered in the Single Mom Handbook.

The dog gave another growly-grumble.

"No. I will not let you in," Alex said as if he understood dog-speak.

The canine drooled and licked the slider, but mostly he panted. Now that the initial shock of him had passed, Marnie noted he had a black nose and a brown mask and ears. He was just so large, white, and Abominable Snowman-like.

"He's thirsty." Alex's death grip relaxed on Marnie's leg. "We have water, doggy." Her little man took two steps toward the slider before Marnie dragged him back.

Panting, the dog plopped to his haunches and tilted his head to one side, trying to see in.

"Mama, you said we have to be nice to the new neighbor."

Their condo shared a backyard and a wall with the unit next door. They'd heard someone move in yesterday. Marnie had planned on introducing herself tonight after whoever moved in had time to settle. But this...

Marnie held on to Alex's small shoulders. "That dog is not a new neighbor. He's a stray." Had to be. There was a no pet policy at the condo complex. She had no problem with people sneaking in hamsters, indoor cats, or parakeets. But this...

The dog rested his humongous head on his humongous paws and made a sound that was half growl/half howl in a way that sounded as if he said, *"But I'm harmless."* And then he put a paw on the glass with all the grace of a ballerina.

Her heart wanted to soften. But Marnie was a single

mother. She had to be strong.

Alex broke away from Marnie's arms and ran to the sliding door. He pressed his hand where the dog's paw was. His small one was almost a perfect fit with the dog's.

Marnie hurried after him. "Touch that slider latch, young man, and you'll never watch Rudolph again."

The beast lifted his head slowly, staring at Marnie with soulful eyes. He licked the glass near her son's face before resuming his panting in a way that sounded like, *"Hot-hot-hot-hot."*

Granted, it was warm. Ninety degrees wasn't too warm for San Diego. But it was warm for the week before Christmas and for a big, furry dog.

"Water, Mama. Please?" Alex had big soulful eyes of his own.

"We're not letting in a stray dog."

An even larger figure stepped on to their small concrete patio.

Shrieking, Marnie and Alex stumbled back.

The setting sun outlined a towering, muscular frame, and kept the man's face in shadow. He surveyed the backyard, paused, and then peered inside as the dog had done.

A second scream caught in Marnie's throat. A man. At her backdoor. With only a flip-lock and a thin sheet of glass separating them.

He moved, and sunlight illuminated him in all his raggedy glory. A sleeveless black T-shirt, faded blue jeans, and tan work boots – torn, dirty, and scuffed. None of which made her pulse slow. Her gaze met his smiling one – blue eyes as soulful as the dog's, his teeth just as white. She wasn't fooled by his good looks and that meant-to-be-reassuring smile. Dressed like that, her money was on vagrant serial killer. The Single Mom Handbook was clear on big strange men in tattered clothing – call the police.

Marnie ran through their small living room/dining area and into the galley kitchen, looking for her phone. Where had she left it?

"Mom?" Alex pointed to the patio.

The man had straddled the sitting dog and was pounding the beast's barrel chest as if it was a drum. "Good boy, Snowflake."

"*Snowflake?*" The name was more fitting for a small white poodle than that monstrosity.

The vagrant serial killer straightened, smiling as if he had the world at his feet. He knocked on the glass.

Did she trust those soulful blue eyes? That sun-kissed brown hair? That sigh-worthy smile?

Alex did. He unlocked and opened the slider.

"Alex!"

"I didn't do anything." Her son's standard disclaimer.

Snowflake bounded in, circling Alex and licking his face, eliciting a giggle. The dog finished with her son and galloped through the living room, past the Christmas tree, toward Marnie.

Big white teeth. Big white paws. Big white underbelly.

He tackled her, knocking the air from her lungs, banging her head to the hardwood, and wiping every trace of makeup from her face with his tongue.

~*~

"Off the nice lady, Snowy." Using the dog's nickname and his cop voice, Jonas Johnson took hold of the St. Bernard's collar and pulled him off the petite woman. "Sorry. He only tackles people he bonds with."

"But…We just met." She wiped her face with the back of her hands. "Tell me you didn't move in next door."

"I did. I was crashing at a friend's apartment, but Snowy wouldn't have fit in that small space."

Introductions were exchanged.

The little boy, Alex, giggled. "You smell like my friend Ursula's Christmas tree."

"That's because I'm managing some Christmas tree lots for my family. We have a big Christmas tree farm. Three generations." He took a couple of weeks off from the police department at the holidays every year to help out.

Holding Snowy back with one arm, Jonas extended his free hand to help Marnie up from her whitewashed hardwood floor. Only then did he get a good look at her – velvety brown eyes, a delicate nose, and a cascade of black, silken hair. Her small hand fit in his like a properly placed puzzle piece. When he brought her to her bare feet, she hardly came to his shoulder. But there was nothing petite about her attitude.

"No dogs allowed." She tossed her hair and tugged at her clothing. Her hair was straight and her body was curvy, covered in blue jeans and a simple red tank top.

Something shifted in the air between them. And it wasn't dog breath. It was a bone deep awareness that spread from Jonas' lungs to his chest to his gut. Her words finally sunk in. "No dogs? In your house?"

"In the entire condo neighborhood!"

"Well, I...Is something burning?" He glanced at the brick fireplace. Was that what had him all tied up in knots?

"*My gravy*." The spitfire hurried into the small kitchen, turned off the stove, and put the saucepan on the back burner. "Ruined again. I'll never get past this."

Snowy trailed after Marnie. He was tall enough to put his nose on the stove, but he didn't. He took deep breaths and then did his doggy-mutter, the one he used to beg for food. He sat, still talking, sounding hopeful and reproachful at the same time.

"Gravy isn't good for dogs," she said. "Especially dogs who aren't supposed to be here." She leaned against the counter, brought Jonas in her sights, and crossed her arms.

"Don't you like Snowy?" Little Alex hugged the St. Bernard. "I do."

Snowy made a soft noise and licked the boy's cheek.

"He talks," Jonas said, studying her for more than just her negative reaction to a dog. "How can you not love a dog like that?"

"It doesn't matter what skills your dog has. He has to go. Little boy. Big dog. Someone's going to get hurt." She touched the back of her head, wincing slightly. "The policy is clear. No pets."

Snowy slumped.

She couldn't possibly care that much about the rules. More likely she didn't want any more overly-loving take-downs or extra-large poop piles for Alex to step in.

"He's not my dog," Jonas admitted. "I'm taking care of him for a friend who just deployed. This was the only place I could find that was available on short notice and had a fenced yard." Yeah, he'd seen the photo of a Marine in dress blues on her corner table next to the brown microfiber couch. And yeah, he wasn't lying. Darren had been deployed with his SEAL team yesterday and was due back in two weeks.

Her gaze flew to the picture in the corner. Something flashed across her face. Pain? Guilt? Remorse? The jumbled emotions disappeared as fast as they came, triggering Jonas' spidey-cop sense. What had begun as a friendly, neighborly distraction, threatened to plunge into private territory Jonas wanted to avoid.

Jonas flashed an expression of his own: his most charming smile – the one that settled speeders he'd pulled over to ticket and that sold Charlie Brown Christmas trees at full price on Christmas Eve. "I'm only here until Christmas Day and then I'm gone."

"So *he's* here until the holiday?"

The "*he*" in question grumbled softly and slid to the floor, putting his head on his paws. Alex sank next to Snowy and gave him another hug.

Marnie shook her head. "Does Snowflake always take things so personally?"

"He's a sensitive dog." Her white granite counter was lined with baked goods, including an open tin decorated with toy soldiers and filled with sugar cookies. "Are these homemade?" He selected a red stocking cookie as she nodded, and then handed one to Alex. The cookie was soft and sweet, worth savoring. "I miss home cooking. Your husband is a lucky man."

Marnie paled.

"Daddy's in Heaven." Alex stood, dropping cookie crumbs on Snowy's head. He bounded over to the couch. "And my grandparents live in Houston and Hackensack."

Somebody liked alliteration.

"Michael's parents are coming to spend the holidays with us for the first time." Marnie's words were tension-filled, her eyes clouded with worry. "They arrive day after tomorrow from Hackensack."

Ah, the reason for the rules comes out.

Marnie glanced at the pot of ruined gravy and then back to Snowy. "Is there anyone else Snowflake can stay with once they arrive?"

"No." Jonas took another cookie and admired the fridge art. If he had to guess, the rectangle with stick legs, Xs for eyes, and a red nose was Rudolph.

"Just for a few nights?" Her voice had a hand-wringing quality to it that reached inside Jonas' chest and squeezed.

How far did she have to reach before she found his heart? Most days lately, it felt like it had gone missing. Some days, like today with an exuberant, friendly dog, it felt merely Grinch-sized.

"My former in-laws didn't approve of me either." Jonas admitted begrudgingly, tugging at his wrinkled, sap-stained T-shirt over the place where his heart should be beating. He was only crashing here for a few days. Why did this have to be complicated? "Hillary's parents wanted someone with a college degree and an office job." Anyone who wasn't a cop.

Snowy climbed onto the couch and curled into a tight ball next to Alex, who leaned on him as if he was a pillow.

"I just…" Marnie lowered her voice, glancing at her son.

"I just want us all to get along and move past...things." Her gaze returned to the photograph of her dead husband. She seemed as reluctant to talk about her past as he was. "Things that...Well, I just want Christmas to be perfect."

Things. Such a small word with such big emotional punch. According to his police captain, Jonas had "things" to get past before he could return to patrol. For the first time in weeks, Jonas felt he wasn't the only person in this oversharing world that didn't want to regurgitate the past. Maybe that wasn't sexual attraction he'd felt when he'd helped her up earlier, but an intuitive emotional connection. Had to be. He hadn't felt anything like it since.

"I could be convinced to take Snowy to work with me at the Christmas tree lot while they're here, if you could see it in your heart to share some of your holiday treats." He gestured to the apple pie and cinnamon rolls on the counter. Both looked homemade.

"Could you?" Marnie perked up. "I'll close the curtains at night so they won't see Snowflake. This will be perfect."

Snowy grumbled and nuzzled Alex's head.

Jonas bit into his cookie. It was bakery quality. Really, setting aside the burnt gravy, Marnie had skills in the kitchen. "So we have a deal?" It was the least he could do for their mutual "thingness."

"We have a deal." And then Marnie smiled.

He hadn't seen her smile before, hadn't experienced that deep hit of joy and enthusiasm.

The air deflated from his lungs quicker than an inflatable snowman with a puncture wound.

This had nothing to do with things.

Chapter Two

"Have a holly, jolly X-mas," Alex sang, kneeling in front of the coffee table where he was coloring in the letters Marnie had drawn on a welcome poster for her in-laws. He used chunky, fragrant markers. "Holly-jolly, holly-jolly." He scratched his nose. Unfortunately, he scratched his nose with the big red marker tip. "Why do they call it X-mas? It's *Christmas*."

"Alex." Marnie weighted his name with maternal disapproval. "Don't try to distract me, young man."

"I didn't do anything." Oh, he had that wide-eyed, innocent stare down.

"You colored half your nose."

"Really?" He grinned and ran to the hall bathroom, presumably to check his reflection in the mirror. "Cool!"

It wasn't cool. Nothing about the impending arrival of her in-laws was cool. She had no idea if they blamed her for Michael's death or had questions about their son that she'd never answered. This could be the worst Christmas ever.

It was certainly shaping up to be the hottest. They wore shorts and tank tops today. All their windows were open and a weak morning breeze wafted in. Just cooking bacon had ratcheted the temperature in the kitchen up. Roasting a turkey in this heat and the pressure of her in-laws in attendance would be like living in Hell's kitchen.

There was an odd tearing noise behind her.

In the hallway, Alex giggled. "Snowy made a doggy

door."

The netting on the slider screen (which – to be fair – had been loose in spots) flapped weakly in the light breeze. Snowflake trotted across the living room. His thick tail batted at the tree and sent an ornament flying. Luckily, it landed in a sparkle cloud of red glitter on the couch. The dog took his place next to Marnie, leaned his upper body against her leg and groaned, eyeing the plate of bacon.

"Bad dog. You can't just walk in here, wreak havoc, and then try to look innocent." The frustration that had ridden her shoulders all morning dug into her temples with spurs. She had a long enough to-do list without adding to it. Why couldn't everything be perfect for Harriett and Rodney? "I thought you were going to work with Jonas."

"Christmas tree lots don't open until ten." Rather than sliding open the screen, Jonas stepped through Snowflake's flap and set a plastic container on the dining room table.

Marnie brought her fingers to her forehead and pressed against her pounding temples. "Can't you use the front door or…or…knock or something?"

"It was open. And we smelled breakfast." Jonas worked a smile like a used car salesman who smelled an impending sale. He knelt to examine Alex's half red nose. "You smell like candy cane."

"Marker." Alex grinned and held up the chunky red pen. He dodged around Jonas to resume his work.

Or color more body parts.

"Very cool," Jonas said.

"It's not cool. None of this is cool." Marnie felt the damn holding her emotions in check bulge and strain to keep her from having a meltdown. She pressed her hands flat on the kitchen counter when what she'd really like to do is slap them with palm-stinging intensity. "Our deal was for baked goods, not breakfast. My in-laws are coming tomorrow, my screen is broken, and you two won't go away."

Jonas let her irritation roll right over him. "You need to relax or things will get to you, and you'll snap." He stepped behind her and massaged her shoulders.

Massaged her shoulders! They'd met less than twelve hours ago. He shouldn't be touching her. He shouldn't be in her personal space.

Marnie opened her mouth to tell Jonas to stop, but then he found a particularly tight, spur-ridden muscle and every cell in her body begged her to shut up.

Too soon, his hands fell away. "The no-dog-allowed clock doesn't begin ticking until the dreaded in-laws arrive." Jonas swiped some bacon. "Crispy. Just the way I like it."

"My screen…" *My shoulders*…She was still in bone-melting heaven.

Jonas shared a piece of bacon with a drooling Snowflake. "You have more to worry about than a loose screen. A Christmas tree says a lot about a person. And this one…" He moved to the four-foot, fake tree and ran his hand over the needles. They dropped as if they came from a real tree. And not one freshly cut. "This tree is small and smells of moth balls. I can see the metal branches."

Marnie snapped out of her lethargy, but didn't snap at Jonas. He was right. How had she not seen it before? The tree she and Michael had bought years ago, when they were young and barely making rent, looked pathetic.

"You want to impress the dreaded in-laws and move beyond *things*…" Jonas confiscated another piece of bacon and her Santa mug of coffee. "You need a tree that says tradition is important to you. And one that says you can afford to provide well for your son."

How could she not have seen this? Every time Michael's parents called, they offered to help her in some way, as if they didn't trust her to raise their grandson alone. As if her failure with Michael made her a less-than-perfect mother.

Snowflake smacked his chops and groaned pleadingly. A puddle of drool had formed at her feet. Pre-occupied working the time she'd need to buy a new tree into her schedule, Marnie gave the dog a piece of bacon.

"What does *dreaded* mean?" Alex asked, looking up from his poster, having added a green soul patch to his chin.

"Favorite," Jonas said quickly with an apologetic smile Marnie's way.

"You're ruining his chances for a high SAT score and a college scholarship." Marnie put more bacon in the pan. It popped and sizzled, reflective of her stress level lately. "Alex, dreaded means – "

"What are you making, buddy?" Jonas studied Alex's work. "Welcome Gammy Harriett and Gampy Rodney. Nice." He slurped Marnie's coffee. "Whew. You like your coffee sweet, don't you?"

The magic effect of Jonas' hands dissipated. "Feel free to make your own cup. At your own place."

Snowflake left the kitchen and joined Jonas in the living room. He sniffed Alex's scented markers, which were strewn all over the coffee table.

"Drool alert." Jonas grabbed a tissue from an end table and blotted the poster dry. He surveyed the damage. "Welcome Gammy Harri and Gampy Rod."

"No." Marnie charged over to look, nearly slipping in the puddle of drool. She'd only bought one posterboard and she'd let Alex scribble on the back earlier. "You ruined it." Did she have time to fight the pre-holiday Wal-Mart crowds one more time?

Not for one sheet of posterboard.

"I didn't do anything," Alex said, innocent for once.

Snowy crept under the dining room table, bumping chairs out of his way.

"Go easy there, sunshine. It still works." Jonas made a high sign behind Alex's back, one that said she was bending and about to break.

At this rate, she'd pick up her in-laws tomorrow and burst into tears, confessing that Michael's death was all her fault. Marnie stared at Michael's picture. "I'm sorry."

"I've heard confession is good for the soul," Jonas murmured. He stood across the coffee table from her, feet firmly planted hip distance apart, thumbs hooked into the pockets of his jeans. If it wasn't for his holey jeans and cut-sleeved gray T-shirt, he would've looked like a cop.

Not that she had anything against cops. But she'd sworn off military men, lawmen, hunters, security guards…basically anyone who toted a gun. And not that she was weighing Jonas on the mating scale. The last thing she needed was a man. Although, after that massage, she'd make an exception for a male masseuse.

"I don't need a cop or a priest." And she certainly didn't

need her in-laws to see her hanging around with someone like Jonas, someone who lived paycheck to paycheck and drove a ramshackle truck that looked like it wouldn't make it down the highway, much less to the grocery store. "I need a fixed screen, a new welcome sign, and a new Christmas tree." She sounded just like her mother.

Nag-nag-nag, her father used to say when a to-do list was produced on his day off.

You like food on the table? Mom would counter. *Take out the trash.*

She gathered the tumultuous emotions swirling inside her and returned to the kitchen to turn the bacon.

Jonas followed her. He rummaged in her cabinets until he found a travel mug. "Salvage the sign." He poured a fresh cup of coffee into it and searched her drawers for a lid. "No one wants to be Grandmother Harriett. Grandmother Harriett never visits and doesn't know how old her grandchildren are. Grandmother Harriett always buys stuffed animals, because she doesn't know her grandchildren well enough to choose something more appropriate."

Alex's lip trembled. It'd been three years since he'd seen Michael's parents. Last Christmas they'd sent him a stuffed bear. It was in permanent time out in Alex's closet, sent there by Alex. He preferred Legos and Hot Wheels.

Jonas continued absently, perhaps distracted by the search for a lid, but he spoke without regard to a little boy's feelings. "Grandmother Harriett drifts across lanes on the road, can't hear an approaching siren, and refuses to give up her right to drive until it's too late."

The heat of the kitchen combined with the desire to

protect Alex pressed in on Marnie until she thought she'd explode. "Are you insensitive with everyone? Or just us?"

"What? I..." Jonas blinked. And then comprehension dawned in his eyes. He hurried to Alex's side. "Hey, I was thinking of someone else's grandmother. She was...She...uh..." His phone beeped. "Crap." He headed for the door with purposeful steps and her travel mug. "Stay, Snowy."

"*Stay?*" Marnie ran after him. "He can't stay. It's against the rules."

Jonas turned and took hold of Marnie's shoulder with his free hand, suddenly serious. "Someone robbed one of my lots last night. I'm going to find them. I can't risk Snowy's safety chasing down thieves." He slipped out the screen flap.

"You're not Batman. Leave it to the police." She poked her head out the screen, biting back platitudes about men who rushed into battle.

"I am the police," he tossed over his shoulder.

Of course, he was. Unflappable. Steady in a crisis. With a license to carry. And didn't that burrow under her skin like an angry fire ant? "Well...I...be careful then. The last thing I need is you in the hospital and me taking care of the Abominable Dog."

"Thanks for caring." Jonas paused at his slider, looking at her with a blue gaze that seemed to understand why she was acting like a whack-a-doo, but not judging her unkindly for it. "I'll fix your screen tonight when I bring you a new Christmas tree." And then he was gone, taking her frustration with him.

She stepped back inside, bumping into Snowflake at her

feet, her knees, her waist. He bodied up to her like a third appendage. Unfortunately, he also shed like her old Christmas tree.

"Unbelievable. I just vacuumed." There was white hair everywhere, enough to make several holiday dust bunnies. "I hate that man." And not because he was a cop.

"You said it's not nice to hate anybody," Alex said, coming to stand on the other side of the big dog.

"You're right." Marnie sighed. "But, I can say he annoys me." And she planned to tell him she didn't want his gun in her house.

"Snowy couldn't annoy anybody," Alex said cheerfully.

"Never." Marnie let more than a trace of sarcasm color her words. "He's a just a dog." He wouldn't tackle someone or make drool puddles or shed enough hair to fill a bed pillow.

Snowflake stared at her with those sad, soulful eyes as if to say she'd misjudged him. *Drat*. She drew a deep breath. She had. Mostly.

She patted his broad head. At the very least, Snowflake would never take someone else's gun and –

"Mama, Jonas is nice." Alex pointed to a plastic container on the dining room table. "He's a good neighbor. He made us cookies."

~*~

"Nathan, how can someone have stolen ten trees when you were sleeping in a trailer ten feet away?" Jonas didn't try to keep the irritation from his tone. Forget that Nathan hadn't been hurt and no money was missing. Trees were a big part of his family's livelihood. Trees might be Jonas' only livelihood if he couldn't convince his police captain he was ready to return to patrol. "Were you drinking last night?"

"No." There was too much force behind the overly-tattooed, young man's words.

The number of trees on the lot matched the tree tally (minus ten) and cash box receipts (minus ten). Jonas took a visual inventory of the tree lot in case something else was missing. The inflatable snow globe stood near a trio of pink flocked trees. An inflatable Santa waved to passing cars.

There were street lights on two sides of the lot. No one could steal ten trees without being seen by a passing car either on the street or the highway overpass a hundred feet away. No one could steal ten trees without being heard. Not without help.

He turned suspecting eyes to his employee.

Nathan flinched under Jonas' cop-like stare. "I'm on probation, man. I have a kid. I want to be home for Christmas."

Home for Christmas. That meant pot luck for Jonas and his four siblings. Laughter with their parents and the grands. A final tally of the year's sales and a toast to future health and prosperity. It meant three generations of cops getting together, thankful they'd all made it safely through another year. Three generations cracking open a beer, talking about their cases, and asking Jonas to relive crashing his cruiser. He couldn't wait.

Cue eye-roll.

Marnie had a different idea of Christmas. She was doing it up the traditional way, with extended family and avoiding talking about things. Granted, the prep for it was tying her up in knots, but there was something about Marnie he liked. Something in her eyes that said she needed a second chance and didn't know where to find it. Certainly not in that fake tree of hers. Alex deserved a bigger tree, one that smelled of the outdoors and Christmas.

Jonas turned his attention back to Nathan. "If I were to look inside that trash can near your trailer, I wouldn't find any empty alcohol bottles or beer cans, would I?"

Nathan blanched, and it wasn't because of the exhaust from passing cars.

Why were all petty criminals such bad liars? "Because if I do, I can't lie to your probation officer. I'm playing golf with him in a charity tournament next month."

The ex-con turned as twitchy as a worm washed to a hot sidewalk. "Give me ten minutes and the beer cans will be gone."

"I'll do better than that. I'll give you two hours – until the lot opens – to call up your drinking buddies and get my trees back." Jonas headed toward his truck, debating whether he should swing by the condo and pick up Snowy or not. He was leaning toward not.

Before Jonas could decide, his cell phone rang. "Captain," he said with false cheer. "Calling early today."

"Johnson." The captain's voice rumbled louder than Snowy snored. "I'm looking at the duty roster for next week. And you're not on it."

He hadn't been since the Thanksgiving crash.

"I've got a question for you." The same question he'd challenged Jonas with for the three weeks since he'd taken leave to manage tree lots. "When a civilian can't hear a patrol car's siren or see its flashing lights, and drives into said patrol car's path, blocking his way during a high speed chase, is it an accident or the fault of the patrolman?"

Jonas gave the same answer he'd given every day for the past three weeks. "It's the fault of the patrolman."

"Wrong answer. Enjoy your holiday, patrolman," Captain Rodriquez said icily. "If a spot opens up on the patrol duty roster, I'll call you. Otherwise, I expect to see you working the desk outside my office come Monday morning."

Jonas didn't see his answer changing. He'd sworn to protect and serve. He hadn't.

And that was his thing.

Chapter Three

"I don't like the smell of those cookies." Alex stared at the round, unfrosted cookies inside the plastic container Jonas had left. He handed it to Marnie.

They'd spent all morning prepping for the Dreads (Marnie's new name for her in-laws). They cleaned Alex's bedroom, bringing the bear the Dreads had given him last year out of time-out, and filling a box with old toys. Mostly Marnie had cleaned and Alex had chattered away, leaning on Snowflake like a big pillow. For his help, Marnie had promised Alex a cookie before lunch.

Marnie took the container and sniffed. "They're gingerbread."

"I don't like gingerbread." Alex traced a finger along the edge of their small, round dining room table, backing toward the kitchen and the two tins of peanut butter kiss cookies. One Marnie planned to take to Mrs. Clinkenbeard in the condo across the way, and the other to her co-workers stuck working the holiday week.

"Alex, you've never had gingerbread." Because Marnie wasn't partial to it either.

Sitting nearby, Snowflake groaned hopefully. He liked gingerbread.

Marnie broke off a piece from one cookie. "I tell you what. You try a piece and then I'll let you have one peanut butter kiss." Sometimes Marnie thought being a parent was one big negotiation. Good thing she excelled at negotiation.

She was the main buyer for the lingerie department at a small chain of department stores in Southern California.

Alex turned up his nose. His sneakers hadn't moved since her offer.

"Come on. Take a bite."

Snowflake stood at the ready. Alex didn't budge.

It was time to make the stakes easier to swallow. "You can give Snowflake the rest if you don't like it."

Alex considered her offer with a five year-old's suspicion. It was hard to keep a straight face when the green soul patch and red nose hadn't completely washed off his face. "You try one first."

Another cookie? She'd probably had half a dozen already this morning.

Promising herself she'd go back to the gym as soon as her holiday vacation was over – even if she had to buy bigger size workout clothes – Marnie took a bite. It was spicy and pungent, less sweet than she expected. Alex wouldn't like them. But she couldn't make a face and give Snowflake the rest of her cookie (even though he had begun a soft whining while she chewed). If she didn't eat the entire cookie, Alex wouldn't try so much as a crumb. And then the next time she put something new in front of him, he wouldn't try that either.

When she finished the cookie, Marnie smiled and held out the piece she'd broken off for him. "Your turn."

"Did you like it?" Alex came forward with reluctant steps.

"I did." It wasn't exactly a lie. She liked it better than Brussel sprouts.

Alex took the piece of gingerbread between his thumb

and forefinger as if it was foul smelling and might bite him back. He nibbled the smallest bite known to man and proclaimed it, *"Nasty,"* tossing it to Snowflake, before running to get a peanut butter kiss.

After lunch, Alex watched TV, while Marnie sat in a lounger on the back porch and checked her work email on her phone.

Snowflake followed her, worming his big head beneath her arm and resting his slobbery chops on her stomach.

"I am so grossed out right now."

He knocked his head at the hand that held the cell phone and emitted a growly-grumble.

"I know. I'm on vacation. I shouldn't be checking email." She did anyway, scrolling through it with one hand while the other stroked his velvety ears. It didn't take her long to finish. Most of her department was on vacation.

Snowflake's cuddling was awfully comforting. A tree blocked some of the midday sun, bathing them in dappled sunlight. Marnie was tired and coming down from a sugar high.

She closed her eyes, thinking about how warm Jonas' smile made her feel, how cold she turned at the idea of a gun nearby, and how relaxed she'd been beneath his touch.

~*~

Footsteps sounded in the grass.

"You shouldn't be alone." Jonas' voice had gotten really husky.

"I'm not alone. You're here." Marnie dragged her eyes open.

Snowflake sat beside her and licked her cheek. Marnie buried her fingers in the thick fur at his neck. Her eyes drifted closed again. "Jonas?"

"He's at work."

She sat bolt upright and twisted around. The deep voice sounded as if it was right in her ear. But Snowflake was the only living thing in the yard, right at her shoulder.

Marnie glanced at her cell phone. She had it set to voice command, and it did occasionally talk when it tumbled around in her tote. But it never said more than, "How can I help you?"

Snowflake put his heavy head in her lap and made a grumbly noise that sounded like, *"He's lonely."*

Now her tank top and her blue jeans were slimed. "I'm still dreaming." Stress dreams. She'd had them after Michael died. This one was just so vivid and lingering.

Snowflake huffed and grumbled something that sounded like, *"You're lonely."*

She gently pushed his head from her lap. "The last thing I need is a man in my life. Or a dog." She went inside, moving quietly since Alex had fallen asleep on the couch, sprawled out like he'd passed out mid-stride in a race. Marnie passed the open tin of gingerbread cookies and took another one, breaking it in two and splitting it with Snowflake. The pungent flavor had grown on her.

She went upstairs to move laundry, Snowflake at her heels.

"Are you making bacon in the morning?"

Marnie stopped at the second floor landing and looked back downstairs. "Jonas?"

Snowflake moved past her and sat in front of the accordion doors hiding the washer and dryer from view. *"I like bacon."*

"Jonas said you were a talker, but now you're talking too much." Darn dream. She was putting words in a dog's mouth. "Don't say another word until Alex wakes up."

Snowy sighed and slid to the carpet, resting his head on his paws. His stomach gurgled and he made a mumbling noise that sounded like, *"Excuse me."*

Marnie opened the doors and dug in the dryer for the towels. "And now I'm talking to myself through a dog. My in-laws are going to think I'm nuts."

Marnie couldn't wait for Christmas to be over and her real vacation – the in-lawless, dogless, Jonasless vacation – to begin.

~*~

"A tree! A tree! A tree!" Alex ran through the flap of the screen into the backyard, followed by a galloping Snowflake, whose panting sounded a lot like, *"He's home! He's home! He's home!"*

Marnie embraced the brief moment of silence. After his nap, Alex had been a chatterbox. And so had Snowflake – groaning, grumbling, and growling in a way that sent Marnie's imagination into overdrive. She'd pinched herself enough times to bruise – she wasn't dreaming. She was beginning to believe she was a dog whisperer, because she seemed to understand every nuanced sound he made. It was either that or believe she'd lost her mind. And wouldn't the Dreads love that?

"Oh, good." Jonas led his pack of males inside, looking just as sap-stained and disheveled as he had the day before – gorgeously sap-stained and disheveled, that is. "You took the ornaments off the tree."

"Snowy and I helped." Alex gave Snowflake a back rub. He'd discovered the dog's ticklish spot earlier.

Snowflake thumped his foot on the floor. *"Ooh-la-la."*

Marnie pressed her fingers to her temples in an effort to unheard that.

"Snowflake tackled the tree," she said in a modulated, sane-person voice. Completely on accident if his grumbly voice was any indication. He'd been in a hurry to be with Alex when he woke up. Marnie very carefully did not look the dog in the eyes for fear of hearing him speak again. "I would have taken it out back, but I started dinner."

Jonas sniffed. "Pork chops?"

"And gravy." Snowflake collapsed on the ground, rolled onto his back and extended his feet in the air. *"Yum."*

"I made enough for you, Jonas." Marnie was in need of some adult confirmation that she wasn't losing her mind. Cops knew the signs of mental breakdown, right? "Please stay for dinner in exchange for you giving us a tree."

Alex hopped across the room. "You should see it, Mama! It's big. Bigger than me!"

Most things were bigger than her kindergartner.

In short order, the old tree was taken out and the new tree was brought in with a minimum scraping of branches against the wall and a minimum of doggy commentary.

Marnie stirred the gravy, flipped the pork chops one last time, and then glanced over her shoulder. *Holy Humongo.*

"It's huge."

The tree blocked the entire path from the slider to the kitchen, from the stairs to the front foyer. It had to be seven feet tall.

"It's perfect," Jonas said. "I don't usually get to pick out my own tree."

"Take it back." Marnie came into the living room for a better look.

Snowflake stuck his head between branches, sniffing deeply.

Marnie knew about dogs and sniffing and what came next. His snuffling snapped the last cord binding her sanity-tested patience. "Don't you dare mark that tree."

Snowflake stared up at her with lazy, innocent eyes. And then he leaned forward, sniffing the tree more delicately this time. *"It smells like wild things."*

"I don't care what it smells like. It's off limits."

Snowflake sat back with a groan. Alex and Jonas stared at Marnie as if she'd sprouted antlers and a glowing red nose.

"Did I miss something?" Jonas asked.

Marnie's cheeks grew hot. "You can take the tree back later. Dinner's ready. Come eat at the counter." The dining room table was a jumble of sparkling ornaments, strands of lights, and gold beaded garland. "I made pork chops, applesauce, mashed potatoes and – "

"Uh-oh." Snowflake sounded like Scooby Do. *"Burnt again."*

Marnie's shoulders sagged. "No one say a word. Please." And by no one, she meant the dog.

She cut Alex's meat into pieces, and then plated dinner

minus the gravy to the soft sounds of Jonas and Alex sitting at the counter. When she turned with their plates, Snowflake disappeared out the slider screen, his thick tail drooping.

"You know, you can buy gravy at the grocery store." Jonas' blue eyes shone with understanding, just as they had this morning.

But he didn't understand. It wasn't just the burnt gravy that had set her off. It was everything leading up to this non-perfect Christmas, including her hearing voices from a dog. Should she admit she was hearing voices?

"It has to be homemade," Alex explained, turning his plate so the applesauce was in front of him. "It was Dad's favorite."

And Marnie had never mastered making it. She made a bowl out of her mashed potatoes and filled it with burnt gravy. Maybe she'd eaten too much sugar lately. Something less appetizing might mute the mutt. "I'm happy to see you didn't get hurt today in your crime-fighting endeavors, Jonas."

"I caught the thief." Jonas gave Alex a sideways grin. "And I didn't trip on my supercape or reveal my secret identity. It was a man who works for me."

"An inside job?" All kidding aside, Marnie had visions of mayhem. She studied Jonas' T-shirt for any signs of a scuffle, and then his face for bruising. The modern day workplace wasn't safe for annual job reviews, much less accusations of theft by a cop. "Did he get violent? Did you fire him?"

"No and no." Jonas couldn't have looked more relaxed if he'd been lying on her couch with the remote in his hand.

"But he stole from you." Marnie built mashed potato

walls to keep the gravy from spilling over. "Workplace violence is everywhere over the stupidest of arguments. Weren't you – "

"No." His grin sharpened almost to a grimace. "I can take care of myself in a fight."

Probably because he had a gun. Probably because he'd never had his gun taken away from him. Probably because he'd never seen his own gun pointed at someone he loved.

"Mama doesn't like violence." Alex speared a piece of meat as if it was a hooked tuna and he needed to kill it. "I can't even have a toy gun in the house. No army men. No light sabers. No fun."

Marnie's stomach lurched. Who would care for Alex if she was mental? The gravy spilled over the edge of potato mountain. Rodney, her father-in-law, had recently retired from the FBI and probably saw no problem giving a boy a toy gun to play with.

"You have a problem with guns?" Jonas glanced over his shoulder at the picture of Michael.

"Yes. And I used to own one." She answered both his questions – the spoken one (guns scared her), and the unspoken one (because of Michael). "How can you trust your employee not to steal a second time?"

"He said he wouldn't do it again." Jonas gave the most cavalier of shrugs.

She envied that shrug. She supposed calm, rational people trusted their fellow man and didn't hear dogs speak English.

"Besides, it's Christmas." Jonas glanced over his other shoulder to the tree he'd brought. "People are supposed to be nice to each other on Christmas."

The branches on the lowest level had to be six feet in diameter. It was beautiful and deserved a room twice as large. "I appreciate the tree, Jonas. It's just too big." Like Snowflake. And Jonas. Marnie liked things in manageable sizes.

"Give me thirty minutes." He smiled. It was the kind of smile that hit women in the gut, the kind they warned about in the Single Mom Handbook, the kind that said, *"Yeah, I'm charming,"* and created mental images of hot kisses on dark nights. "If I don't convince you this is the perfect tree, I'll take it back and get you a dinky one." He caught Alex's eye. "But I'm warning you. The only small trees I have left are flocked pink."

"I don't like them elf size or pink," Alex grinned back. He slurped applesauce from a spoon and blinked at Marnie innocently. "Do I have to take a bath after dinner? I want to help with the tree."

"Yes, you're taking a bath."

Alex's lower lip came out in a small pout. And then he sat up tall. "Can Snowy take a bath with me?"

"No." With her luck, Snowflake would hop in the bathtub and flood the upstairs.

Outside, a dog howled, and it sounded like, *"I'm hungry-y-y-y-y-y."*

Marnie sighed. Maybe she shouldn't fight it. Approach her neurosis with yoga-like calm. Maybe then she'd go back to normal. "Snowflake wants dinner. If you get his kibble, I'll top it with pork chop juice."

"He's not usually so impatient to be fed." Jonas looked

around. "What happened to his dog biscuits?"

Marnie nearly choked on burnt gravy. "His what?"

"The dog cookies I had with me when I came over this morning. Darren gave me a couple canisters, enough to last until he gets back after New Year's."

"Mama." Alex's eyes widened. "You fed me dog cookies?"

"You barely had a bite." Whereas Marnie had a cookie and a half. She might have been recoiling if they hadn't been tasty in their own way. "We thought they were gingerbread."

"I think they are. Darren said Snowy is pretty picky about what he eats."

"Not that I've seen," Marnie muttered.

Snowflake howled again.

"You fed me dog cookies," Alex repeated in a muted tone, as if he wasn't sure whether he should laugh about it or be disgusted.

Marnie scraped the potatoes and gravy into the sink. "At least now you know what they taste like."

Chapter Four

Marnie had been clinging to the stress-ledge this morning, but tonight she seemed about to plunge over the side. She wasn't handling things well.

Not that Jonas was going to do anything about it. If he was off-duty, he didn't talk to people about the things that set them off. And since the crash, he respected the privacy of others even more. So Jonas went started a fire in the fireplace and set up the tree. He cut a few inches off the Douglas Fir's base, and trimmed the branches so it fit in the corner of the living room next to the television. He strung the tree with white lights. He couldn't bring himself to fix the screen. Alex and Snowy loved the flap.

"No bath, Snowflake." Marnie's voice didn't drift downstairs. It broadcast downstairs. "Don't you talk back to me. Out!"

Snowy trudged mulishly down the stairs, and curled into a tight ball on the couch.

"Dude," Jonas said. "You've got to give her some space."

"Are you talking to the dog?" Marnie stood on the bottom step, one foot mid-air, as if Jonas talking to Snowy had stopped her in her tracks.

Upstairs, Alex sang Jingle Bells at the top of his lungs. Only he was creative, and changed the words: *Dog cookies. Dog cookies. Mom ate dog cookies.*

Snowy added a soft, mournful whine to the boy's off-key

notes.

Marnie frowned at the St. Bernard, and then headed toward the kitchen, turning off lights as she went, leaving them in soft, tree-twinkled light. "It's not like I ate them all."

"He's just having some fun," Jonas said, meaning Alex. "Did Snowy behave today?"

"He was...Nothing happened...He just...He talks *all* the time." Her voice bounced in spurts as if she rode too fast over speed bumps. "Do you hear him?"

"Night and day." The dog must have been a politician in another life.

She stood in the kitchen, gripping the counter, enunciating her next words as if she were giving a speech. "No, I mean...Do you understand him?"

Both she and Snowy stared at Jonas as if world peace rested on his answer.

Jonas shrugged. "I guess at what he *says*, same as you."

Both she and Snowy sighed.

Marnie moved to the dining room table and gathered strands of gold beaded garland. "Darren understands him."

"He's Darren's dog. I only have him a couple of weeks, a few times a year." His cop-sense had a grip on his shoulderblades. There was more going on here than a grumbly dog.

She dragged a ladderback chair next to the tree, climbed up, and began draping the string of beads in big loops. She stood not three feet from Jonas, but she felt miles away. That distance should have reassured him – she alone with her things, him alone with his. That distance should have made it easier to back away, thank her for watching Snowy and for dinner, and leave.

But there were the sparkling lights, the crackling fire, the smell of the tree, and Marnie, who looked as if she stood alone in the world.

"When did your husband die?" Jonas blurted, followed almost immediately with, "You don't have to answer that." *As in, please, don't answer that.*

Her hand hesitated mid-drape. "Three years ago."

Upstairs, Alex started another cookie chorus. Downstairs, not even Snowy spoke.

Which was fine. Jonas didn't want to know more. So many men had died tragically overseas. Although…"Was he deployed at the time?" *Could he not keep his mouth shut?*

"No."

Snowy grumbled. Then grumbled some more.

"I know," Marnie said, a bit testily. "I mean, you aren't going to stop asking me about this, are you?"

"You could tell me to go." *Please, tell me to go.*

She glanced down at him and there it was again – that feeling that she was reaching a place inside him. This time, he didn't feel so hollow and his heart didn't feel so small. He couldn't leave now if she asked him to.

Marnie unraveled a twist in the strand. "I don't talk about Michael much," she said, confirming this was her thing, her secret, none of his business. "And the Dreads…" She blushed. "I mean, his parents…"

"You're afraid they'll want to reminisce. And you don't want to rehash things." The same way Jonas didn't want to talk to his captain about why he felt the crash wasn't an accident. Cops were supposed to be able to react in an instant.

Except there'd been nowhere for Jonas to veer off that wouldn't have hurt or killed others. "It's said and done. You can't change the past by talking about it."

She nodded once, tersely. But apparently, he'd opened the floodgates. "He wasn't the same when he came home. He'd seen things." She swallowed, but seemed unable to stop the flow of words – despite how much both of them seemed to want an emergency shut-off valve. "He had nightmares where he fought someone off, where he...I started sleeping on the floor in Alex's room."

She didn't mention fear or bruises or the anguish of betrayal, but Jonas knew. He'd responded to enough domestic violence situations and calls from panicked spouses who could no longer soothe the victims of PTSD.

"We tried different medicines..." She stared at the string of beads in her hand. "He didn't like the way he felt on any of them." Her gaze came to his, tear-filled, distant, anguished. "He turned to other ways to medicate himself. Alcohol. Drugs. And then he stopped coming home at night."

Snowy whined, drawing Marnie's gaze. Jonas grabbed hold of her hand.

"Thank you." She gave a half-hearted laugh that sounded more like a half-hearted sob. "When he was here, we argued. He..."

"Scared you," Jonas filled in, squeezing her hand.

Snowy closed the distance between them and rubbed the side of his face on Marnie's pants leg, leaving a big drooly mark.

"I...uh...changed the locks. He...uhm...He tried to come home. Once."

"Did he die of an overdose?" Jonas knew the answer was no. Most military suicides chose a more familiar method to end their suffering.

"He shot himself." Her voice dropped to a fragile thread. "On Christmas Eve." Those liquid brown eyes sought his. "I'm responsible. I could have done more and made sure Alex still had a father."

Jonas barely knew this woman. Heck, it seemed lately he barely knew himself.

It didn't matter. He drew her into his arms and hugged her with all the tenderness a man with his own demons could muster.

~*~

The best thing about the San Diego airport? No dogs.

It had been a no-neighbor morning. No dog voices. No neighbor mooching food and banging open doors to her past, ones she feared her in-laws would try to open as well.

Jonas had been so nice. The fire, the tree, the tears. He probably thought she was a high maintenance nutcase. Marnie burned with embarrassment. The Single Mom Handbook was clear about breakdowns. Call a tow truck and move on.

So she'd cried on her kind, hunky neighbor's shoulder last night. He was a cop and therefore whatever relationship they had started and ended with six letters – friend. So he hadn't shown up this morning. She didn't need Jonas punching her failure button and she didn't need Snowflake punching her crazy button. She'd punch her own buttons, thank you very much.

"Look at my lipstick, Mama." Alex bounced in a plastic

chair next to her in baggage claim. The chocolate yogurt she'd bought him ringed his mouth like a clown's.

Panic break-danced in her stomach. "Where's your napkin?"

"I threw it away." Alex sounded pleased with himself.

Time was her enemy. Marnie searched through her bag for a wet wipe or a tissue or a stray receipt. Anything to clean his face. Michael's parents' plane had landed. They'd show up at baggage claim any minute.

"Marnie?"

Like now. They'd show up now. With Alex looking untended and his welcome sign a welcome mat at her feet. It had sneaker imprints and chocolate drips, dog slobber and colorful smudges.

Alex stood, tipping his melted chocolate yogurt on his yellow polo. Marnie's fingers found a napkin in her purse. She snatched the yogurt cup, tossed it in the trash, and began a quick wipe – mouth, chest, fingers. Except Alex's fingers reached for the sign before they'd been cleaned.

"Marnie? Alex?" Her mother-in-law looked like a well-kept housewife, too young to be a grandmother. She wore skinny jeans and a flowery blouse. Her hair was a soft brown with softer highlights. She was enviably put-together with an enviable smile.

Marnie and Alex looked liked they'd had a bad day at the circus.

"Look!" Alex held up the sign. "It's my dreaded Gammy Harri and Gampy Rod!" Alex flapped the posterboard in the air and hit Marnie in the eye.

Cover for the D-word.

Squinting, Marnie smiled and went to greet the Dreads. "Harriet. Rodney."

Dutiful hugs were handed out like shots at the flu clinic, even for Chocolate Boy.

Thankfully, the in-laws seemed to overlook the use of the D-word. Thankfully, Michael's parents put on happy-to-see-you smiles. Thankfully, Chocolate Boy wasn't fingerprinting everyone in brown yogurt.

"How old are you now, Alexander?" Rodney had the slim, rigid bearing of an FBI director. His khakis and brown polo seemed impervious to wrinkles. There were wrinkles on his face, though, and silver streaked through his hair. "Four?"

"I'm five," Alex muttered, kicking the dangling posterboard. "I'm Alex and I'm five."

"I brought you this, *Alex*." Harriet dug in her zebra-striped tote and pulled out a stuffed truck. "It has no moving parts and doubles as a nap pillow."

"I'm five," Alex said, reluctantly taking the truck. "And I hate naps."

"He loves it." Tears streamed from Marnie's scratched eye. "Thanks. And here comes your flight's luggage."

"We've got three bags." Up close, Harriet's face had her share of wrinkles, from both the sun and the stress of the moment. "An army-green duffel and two zebra print bags."

"Your grandmother over-packs." Rodney winked at Alex, who eyed Gampy Rod as if he didn't trust him.

"I have a Prius," Marnie said, realizing she should have told them this before. Hopefully, their luggage would fit in her little car.

Be positive. Soldier a grin. Dab at the eye. Christmas will be over before you know it.

"I was so worried you wouldn't want us here," Harriet said in a small voice. "Seeing your tears makes me feel better."

And try to cry. Try to cry with both eyes.

Chapter Five

"Look what Gampy Rod brought me." Alex ran through the living room with a football tucked under his arm, and then froze, striking the Heisman Trophy pose – knee bent up, free hand thrust behind him. "Did I do that right, Gampy Rod?"

"Alex." Marnie drew him aside, taking inventory of the presents under the tree. "Did you unwrap a gift? We're supposed to wait until Christmas."

"No, Mama. I didn't do anything wrong. Gampy had this in his suitcase." He held out the worn leather football.

Marnie glanced up at Rodney as he came down the stairs. They'd been home all afternoon, settling in, and tip-toeing around each other and their unspoken feelings, as if they were wound up Jack-in-the-Box puppets ready to pop.

"It was Michael's." Rodney's smile was like a shadow in a granite statue. A brief trick of the light, gone when you looked a second time. "Let's go outside, Alexander."

"I'm Alex." A half-hearted mumble.

"But you're also Alexander." Rodney opened the slider and followed Alex through. "Your grandmother named your father Michael and I refused to call him Mike or Mikey."

"I called him Mike sometimes," Harriet said softly from the kitchen. Her voice took on a cheerfully fake quality. "I can't believe you baked all this for us. What are these?" She held up Snowflake's gingerbread cookie container. "They're unusual, but tasty."

"Gingerbread." Marnie wasn't going to tell Harriet she'd

eaten dog cookies. "Those are from Jonas. He lives next door." He must have forgotten them last night.

Harriet picked up a sponge and began wiping the counter. "I think my golf girlfriends would like the recipe."

"There's no harm in that." All natural, homemade dog treats probably had high nutritional value. At Harriet's sharp look, she added, "In asking Jonas for the recipe."

Harriet resumed her cleaning. She was either trying to be helpful, was OCD, or didn't think Marnie was a good housekeeper.

The older woman unplugged the toaster, held it over the sink, and released the bottom latch, sending a cascade of breadcrumbs into the sink.

Marnie gripped the back of the barstool. How could she have forgotten to clean the toaster? And why did she just get a whiff of wine? Or was that cleanser?

"It's awkward, isn't it?" Harriet set the toaster back in its place. "Without Michael." Her eyes sought her son's picture.

She and Harriet hadn't spent much time together, only a weekend or two a year during her marriage. Marnie was saved from commiserating about awkwardness by shouts in the backyard.

"Get back, Alexander!" Rodney's stern voice cut through the tension in the kitchen and created a different kind of tension. "Stop! Stay back!"

Familiar, friendly growls drifted in the open windows. *"New people. New people. New people."*

"Don't shoot him, Gampy! Mama!" Alex's voice crested on a wave of high-pitched fear.

"Snowflake!" Marnie's heart did a high-octane

acceleration. "Come here, boy." She ran to the slider just as Snowy veered from greeting Rodney and headed toward the condo. He crashed through the screen flap, tackled Marnie, and sat on top of her, licking her face.

"I missed bacon."

Marnie had never been so happy to be tackled in her life, even if the world spun and looked sparkly.

Rodney stepped through the screen flap, gun in hand.

"Stand down," Marnie wheezed, pushing the beast off her. "He's on our side."

Snowflake pranced up to Harriet and wiped slobber on her skinny jeans. And then he did a happy hitch-turn and galloped to greet Rodney, who'd tucked his weapon into his belt (hopefully with the safety on).

"You promised me you wouldn't bring your gun." Harriet seemed stricken. Everything about her trembled – her hands, her lips, her carefully highlighted and hairsprayed bangs.

Rodney held up a hand. "I'm a Federal agent, Harriet."

"*Retired.* Retired federal agent." Harriet spun away.

Alex hugged the football, looking unsure if he was going to cry or not. "You wouldn't have shot Snowy, would you, Gampy? He loves us."

"I do." Snowflake circled Alex. *"I do. I do. I do."*

For once, Marnie wasn't upset that she heard Snowflake talk. "You brought a gun to our house?"

"He loves them." Harriet's feet pounded the stair treads. "You've ruined everything."

"I'm sorry. Old habits…"

Snowflake sniffed Rodney from boots to belt. *"He's*

scared."

"Scared of what?" Marnie regretted the words as soon as she spoke them. Rodney's eyes had widened and then narrowed suspiciously. Anger spurred through Marnie's veins, overcoming the fear of a gun being drawn near Alex. She shouldn't be under suspicion. She wasn't the one who'd pulled a gun. "Alex, go outside with Snowflake."

When dog and boy left, Marnie put her hands on her hips and confronted her pistol-packing father-in-law. "What are you scared of, Rodney? And don't try lying. I have a really good B.S. detector." A lie. Snowflake was outside romping through the grass with Alex.

"There's nothing wrong with me." His denial and innocent stare were reminiscent of Alex's. "I didn't do anything."

"I didn't say you were defective. I said scared."

The "s" word apparently triggered Rodney's male ego defense mechanism. His chin thrust out mutinously and he crossed his arms over his chest.

"I'm sorry, Rodney – about Michael and Snowy, and about Christmas." Past and present, because this holiday was shaping up to be truly horrible. What if Rodney decided she needed to be locked up for observation at the mental ward? "I have a no gun policy in this house. If you want to stay, the gun goes."

He patted his gun almost absently, as if it was dear to him and he was apologizing for the decision he was about to make. "They asked me to retire last month. Can you believe it?"

Yes. She could. "You know why I can't have a gun in my

home."

He nodded. "You're afraid." His voice dropped low enough to pass state secrets. "I'm…uncomfortable, too."

"But…Of what?" He'd already lost his only child and his job. What else could he fear?

Rodney turned to look at Alex, who was pretending to play football with Snowy. When he spoke again, his words were almost too soft to hear. "Of losing my relevance. Of losing my wife. Of losing the last link to my son."

Marnie's annoyance dissipated. She reached out and put her hand on his shoulder. "You don't need a gun for that."

"I have a portable gun safe." He laid a hand over Marnie's. "I can put it in the attic crawl space, perhaps in the box containing your high school memorabilia." His hand fell away. "I didn't know you played soccer in school."

"And I didn't realize I was a subject of an investigation." Marnie said stiffly. What else had he snooped through? She wanted to howl in frustration. First the screen, then the doggy voice, then the toaster, and now a gun.

"Old habits…"

"It's time for the old dog to learn new tricks – like respect of privacy." Or get his nosey old self to a hotel. Could she do that? It would break Harriet's heart, but she'd do it if Rodney drew his gun again. In the meantime… "How about a gingerbread cookie?"

~*~

Harriet had taken over the kitchen, insisting on cooking dinner. "Join me in a glass of wine, Marnie?"

More likely, Harriet wanted to be near the wine she

finally admitted she'd been sneaking on the down-low all afternoon.

Marnie carried presents she'd wrapped to the tree, kneeling next to the couch. Chances were that Rodney – super sleuth that he was – already knew she'd bought him a "What If?" book by Randall Munroe and a fruit infusion water bottle for Harriet. "I'm not much of a drinker."

Rodney and Alex were putting together a Lego castle on the coffee table. Well, mostly Rodney was putting it together. Alex was humming and assembling a tower of blocks.

"Harriet doesn't like to drink alone," Rodney said, struggling to make a tower cap fit on a corner turret.

Alex took the cap from him and snapped it into place on the first try. "I know how to do it, Gampy." Alex rummaged in the box for more blocks. "I've been to Legoland."

"Excellent." Rodney reached out to place a hand on Alex's shoulder, but hesitated a few inches away, trapped in his fears.

"I'm pouring two glasses, Marnie." Harriet had mellowed out tremendously since the gun incident earlier. And by mellowed, Marnie meant she was buzzed.

"Take one for the team, Marnie." Rodney's hand dropped, and his entire body seemed to droop with it. "You need a college degree to put this together. Drinking would make this impossible for me."

How sad that Rodney feared his feelings more than he did aiming a gun at people. Or dogs.

Marnie reached over, and put Rodney's hand on Alex's back. "Don't let Alex hit you with his light saber."

"We're making a castle." Rodney's voice had a distant

quality to it, but his smile was in the here and now.

"You can't play with Legos without making a sword, Gampy." Alex pulled out a tall, slender tower of linked blocks and waved it about with light saber sound effects. "Especially since I can't make Lego guns."

Jonas and Snowflake came through the screen flap.

For once, Jonas looked ready to be seen in public – combed hair, clean-shaven, wearing a T-shirt not covered in sap. He met Marnie's gaze squarely and without the discomfort a man should give a woman who'd tearfully smeared her mascara on his shoulder the night before. What a guy. Marnie was so happy to see him (a lawman who didn't draw a gun on dogs and snoop in her life), she wanted to stop and stare for awhile, especially since all that male beauty wasn't tarnished by a doggy voice-over.

"I'll fix that screen tonight," Jonas said, not that Marnie believed him. "Welcome to California, folks! How do you like the Christmas tree? It came from one of my lots."

"It's beautiful," Harriet gushed. She had a glass of wine in one hand and a whisk in the other.

Gravy bubbled on the front burner. Marnie slipped into the kitchen and turned the burner down.

"Is this the dog owner?" Rodney stood, introducing himself and Harriet. He shook Jonas' hand. "Sorry about nearly drilling your dog earlier. Rest assured, my gun is now locked away."

"Excuse me?" Jonas sent Marnie a questioning look, labeled urgent, which she deftly refused delivery of. The fewer said about that, the better.

Marnie confiscated Harriet's whisk and stirred the gravy.

"Snowflake shouldn't charge strangers. And by the way, all visitors must heed the sign."

"What sign?" Jonas quirked a dark brow.

Marnie pointed to her fridge artwork. She'd written in chunky red marker, "Gun-Free Christmas. Offenders will have to leave *and* eat elsewhere."

"The old man wouldn't have shot me." Snowflake moved to investigate the presents under the tree. *"He has a dog."*

"Sparky," Harriet said, slurping her wine. "Rodney wouldn't have shot Snowy because of Sparky."

Marnie nearly dropped the whisk. *Harriet could hear Snowflake?*

"A gun?" Jonas scowled at Rodney.

"A dog?" Rodney scowled at Snowflake as he sniffed Rodney's present.

Peace on earth? Goodwill toward man? The holiday was shaping up about as Marnie had expected.

She claimed the extra glass of red wine on the counter and began her interrogation of Harriet to uncover the extent of her dog-whispering abilities. "Snowflake is quite the talker, isn't he?"

Harriet waved her wine in the general direction of Snowflake. "The dog won't shut up. And do you know? He can't keep a secret." She took another drink of wine. "My mother was that way, too."

"A talker?" Marnie checked the wine bottle. It was empty. So much for Harriet wanting a drinking buddy.

"Mom was a snitch. That's how Rodney and I met. My mother was an FBI informant when I was in high school." Harriet stated this with as much pride as if she'd told them her mother had been a presidential frontrunner.

Snowy sat down and stared at Harriet. *"She's bad-ass."*

"White collar crime." Rodney scoffed. "Not as bad-ass as a drug dealer informant, but a brave woman nonetheless."

"You can hear him, too?" Marnie's knees nearly buckled with relief. "You can both hear him." Not a question. Marnie raised her glass in toast. "I thought I was crazy."

"It's a poor joke, if you ask me." Rodney frowned in Jonas' direction.

"Are you talking about the dog...talking?" Harriet frowned. "That's not...he doesn't...It's the wine, isn't it?"

Snowflake did his panting laugh. *"She ate my cookies."*

"Is that dog mocking me?" Harriet paused, the glass midway to her lips.

Yep. "We ate his gingerbread cookies." Maybe Marnie wouldn't have to be lobotomized by New Year's. "The ones Jonas brought over."

"If you're accusing me of putting illegal substances in those dog treats..." Jonas scratched Snowflake behind his ears. "I'm innocent. Darren made them."

"So..." Marnie narrowed her eyes at Jonas. "You never tried Snowflake's cookies?"

"Me? Eat dog biscuits?" Jonas sounded horrified and looked like he suspected Marnie had done all the heavy drinking today.

Snowflake neither confirmed nor denied Jonas' claim. He was distracted by the stains on Alex's T-shirt (ketchup, frosting, chocolate milk). Alex brushed the big dog's nose away, and turned his Lego sword on its side. It became an airplane, complete with a raspberry engine powered by Alex's sputtering lips.

Her son was cute. Everyone should be smiling and staring at Alex. Instead, they were staring at Marnie as if debating what size straight jacket she should wear.

"I was just kidding about the dog." Marnie drank some wine. It dribbled on her navy blouse.

Snowflake gave Marnie the hurt-feelings eye. She shot him back with her stink eye.

"I don't find this amusing." Rodney sat back on the couch. "Whoever's behind this, April Fool's jokes belong in April."

"Are you saying that dog doesn't talk?" Harriet leaned her elbows on the counter, swaying slightly.

Marnie had no qualms about throwing Harriet under the crazy train the two men were driving. She politely tried to change the subject. "I got us tickets to the zoo for tomorrow."

"That's enough wine, Harriet." Rodney gave his wife the cut it sign across his throat. "We all hear the dog. There's a microphone on him somewhere. Come here, boy."

"I don't hear him." Jonas couldn't quite hide his smile. "And if he's wired, he's been wired since I've had him."

Snowflake climbed up on the couch next to Rodney and placed his big head in his lap. *"Search me, Copper. No microphone here."*

Rodney began his inspection with Snowflake's collar, then quickly moved to a full-body search. "Wait until I find it. You'd be amazed at how far technology has progressed."

"Jonas, won't you stay for dinner?" Harriet asked, gripping her wine glass. "We could use a little sanity in the house."

Amen, sister. Marnie might have sent Jonas a pleading look.

"I'd be grateful of a homecooked meal," Jonas said, earning a smile from Marnie.

"Ooh-la-la. That's my tickle spot, Gampy." Snowflake's foot thumped the couch.

It would be fantastic if Rodney found a microphone on the dog, but Marnie wasn't holding her breath. Still, she skipped back upstairs to finish wrapping and change her blouse, because the Dreads had heard the dog speak.

Chapter Six

"How long have you been dating our daughter?" Rodney said as soon as Marnie closed the door upstairs.

"I'm just her temporary neighbor, not her significant other." Jonas sat in a dining room chair and checked Rodney for tell-tale gun bulges. That posture and his clothing were a dead giveaway to law enforcement. But the whole dog-talking thing was weird. For a minute there, he'd thought Marnie believed Snowflake could talk, too. "How long have you been a cop?"

"Forty years. FBI." Rodney gave an answering appraisal. "You?"

"Five years. Temecula P.D."

"But..." Eyes glazed, Harriet set aside her wine. "You said you sell Christmas trees."

"My family owns a large Christmas tree farm. We run several lots in Southern California – San Diego, Anaheim, Riverside, Hollywood. It's a nice break for me at the holidays."

"I didn't catch your last name." Rodney was cataloguing Jonas' features, probably calculating height and weight, and searching for distinguishing scars and tattoos.

"I didn't say." Jonas couldn't blame the man for being protective. Marnie was great. Alex was awesome. But his life wasn't up for a background check, what with the crash and the desk assignment. "I'll be gone Christmas morning. There's no need to use taxpayer resources on me."

Snowy grumbled.

"Yeah, I know, boy." Jonas didn't need to be a dog-whisperer like Marnie to understand what the dog was saying. "The gravy's starting to burn."

"Shoot." Harriet turned back to the stove.

"Are you a ventriloquist? Where's the microphone?" Rodney demanded, pointing at Snowy, who lay across his lap like a blanket. "And why would you pull a stunt like this?"

"You think you're hearing voices from a dog? And you think I'm responsible?" Might want to check your meds, Gampy. No wonder Marnie sounded confused. Her in-laws were mind-muddling. But at least Rodney seemed to have given up on Jonas' background check.

Snowy made a drawn-out, growly-grumbly noise.

"I know." Rodney patted Snowflake. His gaze sliced over Jonas' frame. "I saw the gun, too." He stared at Jonas' pant leg near his right boot. "Didn't you see Marnie's sign?"

Alex stopped dive bombing the Lego castle with his pretend Lego airplane. "Why does everybody have a gun, but me?"

Jonas sat back. He never gave his gun much thought. It was a tool of his trade, like his radio or his cruiser...

His chest felt hollow again. He needed Marnie's soft gaze and warm touch. A hug wasn't out of the question either.

Harriet sniffed the gravy pot. "I don't understand. The gravy always turns out so well at home."

"You don't drink at home," Rodney grumbled as deeply as Snowy. His expression and his voice softened. "This is a stressful time for her."

"Like it's not for Marnie?"

"I wouldn't drink at all if you quit threatening dogs and people with guns." Harriet hit an operatic note that surprisingly didn't shatter glass.

Alex's lower lip trembled.

"Hey, buddy," Jonas said, moving closer to the boy to remove him from his dysfunctional grandparents. "How about you and me go for a walk with Snowy?"

A door opened upstairs. "What's going on down there?" Marnie called. "Why is everyone shouting?"

"Nobody upset her," Jonas whispered, and then raised his voice. "We're fine down here. Just a friendly argument about football – shotgun versus pistol offense."

For once, Marnie's Dreads were silent.

After a moment, the door upstairs closed.

"Alex, everything is okay. We're going to stop fighting now, because…" Jonas pinned Rodney and Harriet with hard looks. "…your mom has been busting her butt to make this a special Christmas." Jonas gestured toward the tree, which was a darn good-looking tree. Having put lights on it, he felt rather proprietary. He hadn't put a tree up in years. "Everyone needs to stop scaring Alex and driving Marnie crazy. Including you, Snowy."

Jonas took the grumbly-mumble from the dog as assent. Seriously, he almost couldn't fault anyone for thinking Snowy could talk. He was that interactive.

"The dog agrees." Harriet looked awed.

"Only because Jonas is a master ventriloquist." Rodney tried to move Snowy out of his lap. No dice.

"This sure beats Christmas in Texas," Alex piped up. "All we do there is ride horses and sing Christmas carols."

~*~

"You look like you could use a drink." Jonas' words, low and smooth, reached Marnie's ears a moment before Snowflake's torso landed on her chest.

"You smell like pumpkin pie."

Because she'd eaten a very small slice before coming outside to sleep beneath the stars. Not that she was going to risk any sanity points with Jonas by explaining that to the dog.

"Down, Snowy." Jonas pulled the dog off her. Snowflake trotted away to patrol the perimeter under the star-sparkled sky.

Marnie drew in a much needed breath. "I get more action from that dog than I did when I was dating."

"You were fishing in the wrong dating pool." Jonas drew up a chair. "When I was younger, I got no complaints about the action I was giving." He extended his long legs to rest on her chaise.

Marnie had been lying on top of a sleeping bag in a pair of long boxers and a tank top. Suddenly self-conscious at his invasion of her space, she sat up and hugged her knees.

His voice…There was something different about it tonight.

Jonas handed her a beer bottle. "You probably prefer one of those fruity wines like Strawberry White Zinfandel, but all I had was beer."

"I'm from Texas. It's a crime to be a Texan and not drink beer."

Neither referred to Harriet's alcoholic preferences.

"Is there a reason you're sleeping out here?" She couldn't make out the nuances of his features in the shadows, but he sounded concerned.

"The living room seemed stuffy." And she'd needed space from her in-laws. She couldn't do anything about Rodney's reluctance to adjust to retirement, but she could clear the air with Harriet tomorrow when the older woman was sober.

"If you need a place to crash, I've got a comfy air mattress next door." There was something wrong with his smoothly charming voice. Jonas didn't proposition her or talk about his dating prowess. He kept it light, but kept it distant.

"What's up with you?" He'd never propositioned her before. If he was propositioning her now. Marnie hadn't dated in so long, she wasn't sure. "More tree thefts?"

"No. I was just talking to…I usually get work calls earlier in the day." He made an audible downshift from a stress-filled voice to a stress-free one. "I need to blow off some steam. Have a few beers, punch someone, kiss a beautiful woman."

She laid a hand on his left ankle. "You don't have to posture with me." She'd had a meltdown on his strong shoulder. They shared a bond, whether he liked it or not. "What's wrong?"

He hesitated too long before answering, changing the subject as deftly as if he'd used a remote. "I've taken an inventory, and it's looking kind of grim around here." The charm was back in his voice, but it was forced and fake. "Your mother-in-law medicates the stress of being here with wine – loved her pineapple meatloaf, by the way – and thinks

Snowy can talk. There's a reason your father-in-law is retired. He's paranoid that I'm a ventriloquist making it seem like Snowy is speaking. And you?" Jonas' voice turned full-on sexy. "I worry about you. You've bonded with a dog that isn't yours. Your heart is bound to be broken when I take him back to Temecula." He paused to drink his beer. "I say we take Alex and Snowy and head for the hills for Christmas."

"Are you asking me to..." She couldn't even say it. Did he think she took him and his come-on seriously? She was smarter than that. Or she would have been if her rusty feminine equipment hadn't come to life with a startled purr. But according to the Single Mom Handbook, she couldn't afford that kind of talk. "You know what I like about Harriet and Rodney?"

"Nope."

She thrust his foot off the lounger. "They're flawed, but they're honest."

"You think I'm not honest?" There were barbs in Jonas' words.

"That's right, *lover boy*." She made her words purr with intimacy as fake as he'd given her. And then she hardened her tone, her expression, her heart. "You're not honest with me or yourself." The breeze picked up, sending a chill down her anger-straightened spine. "At least they admitted they could talk to Snowflake."

"Well, apparently, I didn't eat the doggy treats with groovy, hallucinogenic herbs."

She wished she could see his face. Was there any trace of a teasing smile there? She doubted it, which only fueled her anger. "They're not hallucinogenic."

Snowflake appeared and put his heavy, drooly jowls in her lap. *"Don't fight. He's sad."*

"Did you hear that?" Marnie asked Jonas.

Jonas sat up so fast his boot lugs hit the concrete with a slap. "What? Did you hear a *cat* burglar?"

Marnie clung to the knowledge that the Dreads had heard Snowflake speak.

"He's worried about work," Snowflake said without lifting his head. *"Ask him what he's doing after the holiday. Work-wise."*

She did.

Jonas sat back and said nothing.

Marnie pushed Snowflake's head off her lap. "So you're a cop."

"In Temecula." Nearly one hundred miles away.

"Which means you have a gun." She rubbed her arms against that darn breeze. "Which means you've been bringing a gun into my house since the day we met."

He didn't argue. And Snowflake was unusually quiet.

"I want you to stop." In a handful of days she'd lost control of her safe, gun-free home. "Do you want to know why I don't like guns?"

"Because your husband – "

"No!" Jonas, her dreaded in-laws, the dog that made her doubt her own sanity. Marnie's body trembled with the need to lash out, to strike back, to be understood.

She swung her feet to the ground next to his. A cop could take the details. She wasn't sure Harriet could. "Because my husband came by one night and broke in the slider. Because my husband came upstairs to the bedroom while I was sleeping the exhausted sleep of a single mom and took the gun he'd bought me out of the gun safe in the nightstand." Who knows what he'd thought about doing as he stood over her. She swallowed back the throat-choking fear, as fresh as if it'd happened last night, not three years ago. "Because my husband went into our baby's room and woke him up. Alex called for me, thank God." Thank God, thank God, thank God. "We were lucky. There was still some of the man I married inside him. I talked Michael out of putting *us* out of *his* misery. And then he walked down to the corner gas station and shot himself by the dumpster with *my* gun."

Marnie gripped his knees, his solid, grounded knees, wishing she could as easily get a grip on her emotions. "I could have helped him more. I could have been more supportive and soldiered through. That's what military wives are supposed to do, right? Not get scared and lock him out of the house." She leaned her weight on her hands, leaned on him, reaching for his strength. But whatever he offered, it was only temporary. He carried a gun. That meant she couldn't let him in her life long term. Her voice dropped to a strained whisper, one that didn't sound like her at all. "I could have gotten rid of the gun, too. But I thought it was my last defense against him. Instead, it was what did him in." How naïve she'd been. It'd almost cost Alex his life. "I'll never keep a gun in my home again."

In the distance, a car went too fast around a corner and a dog barked. And then there was silence and darkness and an aching guilt that seemed like a hard plastic bubble around her heart.

But oddly, it wasn't as painful of an ache as it had been

before.

"First off, you had your weapon in a gun safe. Only someone who knew the combination could get it. Secondly, you have to know that Michael would have found someone else's gun, if not yours." There was anger. Perhaps regret. He set down his beer and laid his hands over hers.

"He has to say it."

Marnie had her mouth open to argue his points, but something in the dog's tone gave her pause. Jonas had mentioned a work phone call. He wasn't his normal, supportive self. And work...? "Are you on suspension or something?

His hands left hers. He sat back in his chair.

Snowflake panted.

Marnie sensed this was important. Whatever Jonas wasn't saying. And if he didn't say something now, he might never open up.

Or he'd open up to someone who had no issue with guns.

Marnie released his knees and gripped the edge of the lounger instead, suddenly feeling off-balance. She didn't want Jonas – who was great with Alex and loved Snowflake – to go to someone else with his problems. "I don't know what's happening here," she whispered. "Did you...Did you shoot someone?" Why else were cops put on leave?

"Would it matter if I had?" His voice was raked with guilt and gravelly with pain.

"No, I..." What was she saying? She was as anti-gun as a woman could get. "Do you want to talk about it?"

Snowflake stopped panting.

"I didn't come out here to talk about the things in my

past or yours." His voice barely reached her, as if he didn't want her to hear what he had to say. But then it gained in strength. "I didn't come to make confessions or hear yours."

"He has to say it."

"I know," Marnie said, suddenly exhausted. "You keep it all inside, the same as Michael. But the things you try and hide can eat you up in sharp, tiny bites." Guilt had certainly made Marnie's gut its own personal buffet. How odd that it had taken this man to make her realize it. "Whatever's bothering you – *about your life or your work* – you came out here because you didn't want to confront it. You didn't want to be alone."

But he would be alone. He'd leave and go back to Temecula, and nothing would change. She so did not want to be like him. She'd had enough of holding it all in.

"I don't care about being alone." His rejection sounded like it came from a hurt place deep inside him. "I came out here because I can't stop thinking about you. I came here for this." He pushed Snowflake aside, leaned forward, and kissed her.

It wasn't a tender kiss. It wasn't a passionate kiss. It was a lonely kiss, a punishing kiss, a desperate kiss.

His breath was ragged. His body hot as a raging fire. His hands gripped her arms, fingers digging into her flesh.

She'd never been kissed in such a way, as if he wanted her, but despised himself for wanting her.

She relished being punished. She accepted his heat and his anger and his desperation and gave back equal measures of her own. It felt good to let the darkness out.

Snowflake bumped between them. *"Enough already."*

Jonas sat back, his face in shadow. Was he shocked at what he'd done? Disgusted? Angry? She couldn't see. She couldn't sense.

Marnie's hand came up to her damp lips. She felt hot and numb, thrilled and appalled. She had to take inventory: *Limbs? As pliant as rising bread dough. Stomach? In upheaval. Heart? Revving like a NASCAR engine.*

Dazed, she didn't realize Jonas had left her until Snowflake mumbled something that sounded like a curse and bounded away.

Head? Full of regret.

Chapter Seven

Someone knocked on Jonas' front door.

Snowy sat up with a tentative woof. And then he trotted
from the living room, where Jonas had set up his inflatable
mattress and sleeping bag.

It was nearly midnight. Jonas hadn't been asleep. He'd
been thinking about Marnie, and his job in Temecula, and
Marnie, and the last day of tree sales, and Marnie.

What kind of idiot kissed a woman the way he'd done?
Without tenderness or warmth?

He grabbed his gun from beneath the mattress and
followed Snowy to the door. Maybe it was Marnie.

Someone knocked again. "Jonas?" A man's voice.
Rodney's voice.

A glance through the peephole confirmed it was Marnie's
father-in-law. Alone. Jonas opened the door, his gun in his
hand behind his leg. He was, after all, a cop. And Rodney had
been, after all, erratic earlier.

"Can I come in?" Rodney glanced past him into the dark
condo.

"Why?"

"I think I owe you an apology." He had his empty hands
at his sides and didn't shift a muscle in his stance.

Jonas opened the door wider.

"I let the whole situation with the dog upset me." Rodney
sounded sincere as he walked in. He flipped on the kitchen
light and took in the condo that was a mirror image of

Marnie's, minus furniture, decorations, and the feeling of home. "It looks like you're squatting here."

"I could either fight the traffic ninety minutes each way, or I could live like a transient." Two-hundred fifty bucks later, he was happy with his choice.

Snowy took a sitting position between the two men, like a referee with two boxers in the ring. He grumbled softly.

"I overheard you talking to Marnie earlier." Rodney's silver-brown eyebrows set in a grim line.

The guy really had problems with letting go of the G-Man life. Spying on his daughter-in-law? Unbelievable.

"I didn't mean to eavesdrop," Rodney said, as if reading his mind. "I was getting a glass of water for Harriet." The older man shifted on his feet, discomfort oozing from him like sap from a scarred tree limb. "Marnie never told us about Michael breaking in. I mean, I knew she'd kicked him out, and I had my suspicions about – "

"Him getting violent." Jonas had no problem setting the record straight if it helped Marnie find peace. "I don't know the details, but she implied he was violent at least once." The thought tore him up inside with those sharp, tiny teeth Marnie'd told him about. "She blames herself."

The eyebrows went up. "She shouldn't."

Snowy made a short, sympathetic whine.

"Agreed," Jonas said. Times ten. Marnie was more sensitive to the feelings of others than most people Jonas knew, which probably explained why she could read Snowy so well. "And I think she believes you blame her, too."

"We'd never…In fact, we feel we could have done more." Rodney ran his fingertips back and forth on the black granite countertop's edge. "We all carry guilt. And maybe our actions or inaction or delayed actions contributed to my son's tragedy, but ultimately…" His words echoed in the nearly empty space. "None of us can say we killed him."

"Wise words, sir." Deserving of a respectful response. "I'm sure Marnie would love to hear them."

Rodney gave a slow nod, seeming to choose his next words carefully. "Sometimes even when we hear, we don't listen." He placed a hand on Jonas' shoulder. "Like when a man risks his life upholding the law and someone dies, through no fault of his own."

Jonas went as cold as the time he'd fallen into Big Bear Lake on a snowy Christmas Day.

Rodney had run a background check on Jonas, probably based on his truck's license plate.

Rodney had talked to Jonas' supervisor, which explained the late night call from the captain, the repeated question, the same answer as before. The patrolman was responsible. Only this time, the answer had clawed through his veins, until all he wanted was relief. And the only relief he wanted was to be in Marnie's arms.

Jonas shrugged off the older man's hold. "Get out."

Snowy only had eyes for Jonas.

"You know that old woman should have given up her driver's license years ago. Her family should have reported her to the DMV or done something to get her off the road. The world is lucky she didn't plow through a morning school crossing."

Jonas' jaw popped, but the ice within him didn't thaw. "Are you saying I did the world a service when I killed a great-grandmother during a high-speed chase?"

"No. I'm saying ultimately, there are probably five or six reasons her car found its way into your path that day. You are not a murderer." He reached for Jonas' shoulder once more, but Jonas stepped back. "You and I both know a murderer has intent to kill. Did you see her vehicle and take aim?"

"No, sir," Jonas said tightly, clenching his fists.

"Did you want her to die?"

"Hell, no, sir!"

"It was an accident. A tragedy. Just like what happened to my son. Don't make light of it, but don't carry the blame on your shoulders alone." With a tight nod, Rodney headed toward the door.

Jonas hadn't thought about the event in that light. He'd talked to a counselor. He'd talked to his friends in the department. No one had put this perspective on it. It was so strange, so different, that Jonas couldn't immediately accept it. "Sir...*Rodney?*"

Hand on the doorknob, the older man turned.

Jonas couldn't accept it, but perhaps someone else could. "Marnie's more deserving of your speech than I am."

"I don't think so, but I'll talk to her."

~*~

"Wake up." A now familiar tongue laved Marnie's cheek and ear.

"Snowflake." Marnie pried her eyes open and immediately covered her eyes with her hands to shade her bloodshot orbs from the rising sun.

"Bacon?"

Marnie peeked through her fingers. "Please tell me Jonas is standing there."

"Bacon?"

Nope. No Jonas. She was still a nutcase. If the in-laws weren't here, she'd have checked herself into an emergency room to protect Alex by now.

"Marnie?" Harriet's voice carried through the screen.

Marnie swung her feet to the ground, sending two empty beer bottles clattering to the concrete.

"There you are." Harriet peered through the screen. "Is that the Snowman?"

"Uh-oh. Bed-head." Snowflake tilted his head for a better view of Marnie's hair.

"What?" Marnie did a quick finger comb.

"I said…" Harriet came through the screen flap and stepped onto the patio. She'd showered and dressed and looked like a sober New Jersey housewife with a hangover. Her squinting against the sunlight only increased the impression. "Is that the Snowman?"

"Still got bed-head." Snowflake licked the hair behind Marnie's ear and then drew back to look at her with those I-see-everything eyes, doing the pant-pant equivalent of doggy laughter. *"Lost cause."* He trotted to greet Harriet, who welcomed him with open arms.

"Are you alone?" Harriet gazed around the backyard. "I thought I heard a man's voice."

Snowflake sat and did his panting laugh. *"Been too long since she ate a cookie."*

Or had a drink. "Snowflake's doggy voice sounds like English, doesn't it?" Marnie stood, straightening her pajamas and reaching for her hair, which felt like a skein of tangled yarn, despite Snowflake's slobber. A shower was definitely in order.

Marnie tripped over a beer bottle.

Harriet stopped petting Snowflake and frowned in disapproval, the pot calling the kettle black.

"Oh." Marnie picked up the empties. "Jonas – *from next door?* – we shared a beer last night."

Harriet's speculative gaze might just as well have asked, *"And then what?"*

"Jonas and I just met." *Not making this any better.* "And I almost never drink." *Head thunk.* "In fact, I've been thinking about making a sign for the fridge. Alcohol Free Zone until New Year's Eve. What do you think?"

"Do you think that people…" Harriet swallowed. "*That I* need a sign?"

Yep. But it was better to lie. "Who? You? No. My head hurts from that beer." Really, it was from lack of sleep. Something was eating Jonas, something that made him kiss her as if the devil himself made him do it. Would he have kissed her at all if something at work hadn't set him off? Did she want him to kiss her again? It made Marnie's head ache. "Doesn't your head hurt, too?"

"No." Harriet put a hand over her chest dramatically, as if offended that Marnie would think she'd be hungover.

Snowflake released more panting laughter.

"It's not funny," Marnie whispered as she walked past the dog, using the loose screen like a tent flap to get inside. Water was running in the shower upstairs. She'd have to wait to get clean.

Harriet followed her in. "What isn't funny?"

"A dream, Harriet. I had a bad dream." She was living in a bad dream.

"Nice save." Snowflake ambled beside her.

"Go home, Snowflake." Marnie pointed toward the door. "Out."

He sat. *"What? No bacon?"*

"What did you dream about?" Harriet asked, patting Snowflake's broad head as she went into the kitchen. "I excel at deciphering dreams, and we'll have time to talk about yours while I make breakfast."

"This should be good." Snowflake followed Michael's mother to the edge of the kitchen. *"It smells like bacon in here."*

Why lie more than she had to? "I dreamt Snowflake could talk. And he wouldn't shut up or go home. Don't you remember we talked about this last night? Before dinner? Rodney thought Jonas was a ventriloquist."

"Things get fuzzy when I..." The older woman's cheeks pinkened.

"Go easy on her." Snowflake sat at attention at the kitchen entry. *"There's bacon on the counter."*

"Bacon is fattening." Marnie headed for the coffeemaker. Bless Harriet for making some.

The dog pouted at Marnie with big brown eyes. *"Jonas likes bacon, too. And he's still sad."*

Jonas was a lot of things, all trapped in the dark depths of his soul behind the façade of easy going charm. Had she touched a nerve when she'd told him the truth about Michael? Or was he a seething mess?

Given the way he interacted with Alex, she doubted Jonas seethed.

She was the one who was a mess. She heard a dog speak. There was a gun in her house. And heaven help her, she wanted another kiss.

Harriet laughed. "If you didn't want bacon, you shouldn't have put it in the fridge. But back to your dream. They say holidays are the most stressful time of the year. What could a dog represent?"

"I bet she reads her horoscope every day."

Marnie glared at him.

"Except for his head, Snowflake is white as a ghost." Harriet met Marnie's gaze. "He must represent Michael. He had a glorious sense of humor. And he loved bacon." Harriet tapped a packet on the counter and smiled at the dog. "I bet you want some of this."

"Now we're talking." Snowflake gave her a toothy grin.

Marnie got herself a glass of water and two Tylenol. Only then did she pour herself a cup of coffee, doctoring it with cream and sugar.

Harriet used Marnie's water to take Marnie's two pain pills. "I...uh...I'm not so nervous today. What about you?"

"It's Christmas Eve, Harriet. How can we not get along on Christmas?" Marnie could make a list. Instead, she refilled the water glass and shook out two more Tylenols.

Jonas entered through the screen flap and stood inside the door. He didn't have bed head and he wasn't wearing slobbery-streaked pajamas. He wore a blue Imagine Dragons T-shirt and jeans that had seen better days. "Merry Christmas Eve." His gaze sought out Marnie's.

In his blue eyes, she recognized regret and apology and wanting. It was the wanting that scared her the most, a feeling that constricted her chest. She hadn't let herself be close to a man, much less want him in years. Logically, she knew Jonas had a valid point about the gun safe. It was just...fear gripped her stomach.

"Can I talk to you?" Jonas held out his hand.

"Not before we do." Rodney stood on the bottom step of the stairwell.

Jonas frowned. It wasn't a what's-going-on-here frown. It was an I-don't-trust-you frown. "Let's all sit at that table."

Marnie had to gulp in air before she could speak. "What's going on? Did someone die?" Someone Jonas, Rodney, and Marnie knew? There was only one person they all knew besides Marnie. And then the fear really struck, hard enough that she could only squeak out the words, "Where's Alex?"

"He's in the shower. He said big boys take morning showers." Rodney gestured to the dining room table. "Come. We want to talk about Michael."

Marnie was breathless with relief, and then breathless with apprehension. Snowflake bumped his head beneath Marnie's hand, as if realizing she needed moral support.

"Michael?" Harriet said in a voice knotted with tension.

Rodney nodded. "And since Jonas didn't know him – "

"He needs to stay." Snowflake gazed up at Marnie with pleading eyes.

" – Jonas should give our family some private time."

"He needs to stay." There was an urgent pitch to Snowflake's voice that Marnie had never heard before.

"Jonas stays," Marnie said.

Glances were exchanged between the men. Marnie couldn't decipher their significance.

"Come. Sit." Rodney gestured toward the table, but his words were given in sharp doggy commands.

Jonas came to Marnie's side. He smoothed her hair. "You might want to find a comb. Or pop in the shower." His teasing tone. His light smile.

Marnie needed them. She took his hand. "I'd like to stand. I know we all loved Michael, but I have some hard things to say."

Harriet sank into a dining room chair. Rodney stood behind her, hands on her shoulders.

"I loved him," Marnie said simply, standing between Jonas and Snowflake, two pillars of strength. "But when Michael was discharged and Alex was born, it was all I could do to work and pay the bills and care for Alex." Her mouth was dry. She had to work up some saliva to continue. "And Michael…Well…I should have done more for him, especially when things became grim." Marnie looked from Snowflake to Jonas, from soulful brown eyes to sorrowful blue ones. "Because of me – "

"We have an intelligent, engaging grandson because of you," Rodney said firmly. "Don't think you're alone with your guilt. Harriet and I feel we let Michael down, too." He stood rigidly behind his wife. "There's no one here to blame for the way our son's life ended. On this day, the anniversary of his passing, I don't think Michael would want us to grieve over might-have-beens."

Harriet sniffed and reached up to cover one of Rodney's

hands with her own.

"Well said." Jonas released Marnie's hand and put his arm around her.

Marnie fit against him with a sigh, drawing from his strength.

"Forgiveness takes time." Rodney stared at Jonas as if this message was meant to include him as well. "It's the season to forgive ourselves as well as others."

"Love is forgiveness." Snowflake leaned against Marnie's leg, depositing a small puddle of drool on her bare foot.

"I forgive everyone in this room," Harriet blurted. "I don't want to know the details. We're all good people here."

Marnie stared up at Jonas. His brow was clouded.

It struck her then. The truth of what was eating him. "You don't think you're a good person."

His eyes widened slightly, but he didn't defend himself.

Marnie's skin prickled the way it did when too many emotions struck at the same time. "I've felt guilty for years that Michael killed himself with my gun – "

Harriet blanched. *"Please…"*

" – but I never considered myself a bad person because of it."

Jonas' face hardened. His jaw clenched. His lips met and thinned. And his eyes sought…

Rodney.

Marnie's insides turned, the same as they'd done when she'd learned Michael was dead. "There's something going on here. Between you two."

Harriet glanced up at her husband. "Yes, there is."

Upstairs, the shower stopped. Any minute now, Alex would be running downstairs.

Marnie glanced at Snowflake.

"He has to say it."

Marnie turned to Jonas, feeling a sudden urgency, as if Jonas had something she needed, but he was slipping out of reach, taken away by a riptide, drowning alone. "I trust you. I know we've only known each other a few days, but…I trust you."

He'd taken a step back. His eyes seemed to be taking inventory of her, imprinting her into his memory. It was the same look she'd seen in Michael's eyes that last time.

Marnie held out her hand. "Don't go. I've told you things. Things I've never even told them." Marnie glanced at her in-laws. There'd be time for apologies and explanations later. "Whatever it is, you can tell me."

Jonas took another step back.

"It's the cop curse," Harriet whispered. "They carry things around, dreadful things, things they think those they love can't handle, and it eats everyone up inside." Harriet got up and went to the kitchen, looking like she needed a drink.

Rodney's expression was as cold as carved marble. He stared after his wife.

"Don't go, Jonas," Marnie said. But her words were a plea to the empty space where he'd been standing moments before.

Snowflake went to sit at the entry into the galley kitchen.

"Aren't you going to follow him?" she asked, uncaring of what the Dreads thought of her talking to a dog.

"Only he can say it." Snowflake followed Harriet's

every move.

Marnie's chest hurt. There was an unexpected hole in her heart. When had Jonas worked his way in there?

"Where is a frying pan?" Harriet's voice skittered along the ceiling as she banged cupboard doors.

"Here. The pans are right here," Marnie said softly, showing Harriet a cupboard she'd just banged around in. "Please, I…I want you to feel at home." She glanced at Rodney, who'd sank into the dining room chair Harriet had occupied. "Both of you."

"She has made herself at home." Snowflake tilted his head to regard Harriet. *"I saw her move your tree ornaments earlier."*

Marnie glanced at the tree, noticing a few ornaments weren't where she'd placed them originally – a New York Mets ball (Michael had been a fan), a leg lamp from A Christmas Story (a gift from Harriet), and a miniature picture of Michael holding Alex in the delivery room. All three had been put front and center. Marnie felt a bone deep warmth. Impulsively, she hugged Harriet.

"We come with baggage." Harriet held the frying pan, looking as if she'd like to wield it at someone. Hopefully Rodney and not Marnie.

"I could fit four bags in my Prius," Marnie said, trying to lighten the mood.

"When I get nervous or stressed, I drink." Harriet held her head up high. "I don't like being on anti-depressants, so I tend to stay within the familiar."

At least, Marnie knew where Michael came by his aversion to medication. She glanced at Rodney to see if he gave any indication that Harriet's self-medicating was a bigger problem than she made it out to be. He was staring at his hands and nodding.

Upstairs, Alex opened the bathroom door and ran to his room, feet pounding on the floor boards.

"Rodney has made his career his life." There was a snippy sadness to Harriet's words. "They forced him to retire and he doesn't know what to do with himself."

Rodney was still nodding.

So far the baggage hadn't been much more than a small carry-on.

"And I want to have a baby."

Ka-boom! Oversized luggage at check-in counter #5.

"You're uh…And he's uh…" Marnie felt as if she shouldn't be a part of this conversation.

"Rodney is sixty-five, twenty years older than I am." Harriet crossed her arms over her chest. "I had Michael when I was young."

This…I did not know. Marnie had always thought Harriet was well-preserved, not that young. But she'd said something yesterday about meeting Rodney in high school.

Was it inappropriate to suggest Harriet get a cat?

"But I would like to offer a compromise." Harriet's nose rose in the air. "I'd like to move to San Diego to help raise my grandchild."

"Could she cook bacon now?" Snowflake nudged Marnie's hand, drawing her gaze downward. *"No one's making bacon."*

Rodney stood, love radiating from his tender smile. "This, I could do."

Harriet blew him a kiss, and then banged the frying pan on the stove. "I'll have bacon cooking lickety-split."

Snowflake blinked at Marnie. *The ornaments look better where the old lady moved them.* He ambled over to the slider. *"I'll be back in time for bacon."*

Alex bounded down the stairs. "It's my dreaded Gammy Harri!"

Harriet jerked and froze, her hurt gaze seeking Marnie.

"He thinks dreaded means favorite," Marnie was quick to explain.

"It doesn't," Harriet said in a hollow voice.

"It doesn't," Rodney said sternly.

Alex threw his arms around Harriet's legs.

The tense, guarded expression on her face softened as she drew Alex closer, her eyes filling with unshed tears. "Michael used to hug me like this."

Marnie wrapped her arms around Harriet. No matter what happened with Jonas, this Christmas and Marnie's family were going to be all right.

Rodney joined them in the kitchen, encircling them all in his embrace.

"I hug Snowy like this." Alex grinned up at Marnie. "Dogs are people, too, you know."

Chapter Eight

Nothing was wrong.

Nothing.

It wasn't as if Jonas didn't have a job. It wasn't as if he was broken and contemplating his own demise. And his family? His family was healthy. He was healthy.

So why did the empty hull of a man that was Jonas Johnson feel different today?

Because he didn't want to be an empty hull of a man.

He didn't want to go through life skimming the surface, closing off memories, keeping people at a distance.

And by people, he had to be honest with himself, he meant Marnie.

I could have done more and made sure Alex still had a father.

Jonas saw again the white Buick pulling slowly into his path, swinging in a wide arc, blocking lanes of traffic and making a very large target. Her pale white hair, her pink powdered skin, her crimson blood.

"I killed her." He whispered the words he'd never said aloud. But there were other words pressing his chest, bubbling to his throat, needing to be voiced. "Why didn't you see me?"

A black and white SUV with flashing lights on top and a high-pitched siren was hard to miss, especially when the rest of the vehicles had pulled aside. She'd never turned to look. She'd never seen him coming.

Jonas sat on the fireplace hearth, listening to the indistinguishable murmurs coming from Marnie's condo next door, and wanting to be there more than he wanted to be here. But there was Rodney, who knew exactly what happened. And there was Marnie with her declaration that he wasn't a bad person. And here was Jonas, wanting to believe.

Snowy slipped in the open back slider and came to sit in front of Jonas, staring into his eyes.

Marnie believed in Jonas. She believed he wasn't a bad person. She believed a picture perfect Christmas would make everything all right.

He ruffled the St. Bernard's hair. "I could use a little Christmas magic."

Snowy sighed, and leaned into Jonas' hands, and leaned…until he collapsed on to the carpet. Jonas could see why Darren loved the dog so much. It was as if he understood every conversation. He certainly participated.

Snowy stretched his nose toward Jonas' cell phone, giving it a tentative lick.

Jonas picked up the phone and studied Snowy suspiciously. "Did Rodney put you up to this?"

The dog groaned a few times and rolled onto his back, but he watched Jonas the whole time, watched him unlock his phone, watched as he dialed the captain.

"Thanks for checking in, Johnson." There was too much satisfaction in the captain's voice. "What a surprise."

This might have been a mistake. Jonas felt as if he was calling his probation officer.

"Talk to me, patrolman."

He should say he was ready. He should say he felt like a

confident, competent cop. Not like the cop who hit an ancient Buick with his cruiser during a high speed chase and killed a great grandmother who should be celebrating the holiday with family.

A family he'd apologized to. A family who'd said they'd understood. That Grandmother Dorothy had been fiercely independent. No one in the family was close enough to her personally to have swayed her to stop driving. Grandmother Dorothy. Not Granny Dot.

Self-forgiveness was what he needed if he had any chance with Marnie.

Forgiveness takes time.

"Patrolman?"

Ultimately...none of us can say we killed him.

Rodney's words echoed in his head. Could Jonas believe him?

I never considered myself a bad person.

Marnie's words echoed in his heart. Could Jonas absolve himself?

His captain didn't think he was a murderer. He'd seen the dashboard film and agreed that swerving to the right or the left would have injured and possibly killed more civilians.

His family didn't think he was a murderer. They considered it an accident.

Rodney didn't think he was a murderer. He understood how a series of unfortunate events could lead to devastation.

Marnie didn't think he was a murderer. She took him on faith. Much as he'd done from the moment she'd mentioned "things." What would it be like to have someone like her to come home to every night? Someone who thought the best of others, even when they doubted themselves?

"Sir, the crash I was in? It was an accident." It was a tough concept to embrace and he'd never let go of the guilt, but Jonas finally believed it was the truth. "And a tragedy."

"Yes, it was. An accident and a tragedy," the captain said, his voice no longer brusque. "I couldn't send you out on patrol again with you doubting your decision-making ability. I'll see you have a spot on the patrol duty roster on Monday."

Jonas hung up the phone. "An accident." The words felt less like a cop-out and more like the truth.

Muted laughter carried on the wind from one backyard slider to the other.

Jonas wanted to explore a relationship with Marnie. But she had a no gun policy. Cops had to carry their weapons to and from work. He was dealing with things. She'd dealt with things with her quirky, dreaded in-laws. But on the gun issue, he was certain she wouldn't budge.

"It's hopeless," he said to Snowy, hating that his words rang with finality. "Well, we better get to work." It was the last crazy rush before the holiday.

The dog padded over to the stack of cookie canisters on the kitchen counter. Snowy looked over his shoulder at Jonas, almost with disdain.

"Okay, I'll give you a Scooby Snack." Jonas gathered his keys and locked the slider.

The pungent smell of gingerbread assailed Jonas as soon as he flipped open the lid. He handed a brown cookie to Snowy. Marnie had mentioned everyone had eaten a doggy treat, except him. Rodney had never found a logical answer to the dog speaking to them.

The St. Bernard tilted his head, refusing the cookie. And then looked from the canister to Jonas.

"Oh, no. I'm not eating dog food."

Snowy sat and groaned.

"I don't have time for this. Eat this or I'll put it back."

Again with the intense stare.

Marnie loved this dog. And the dog seemed to love her back.

But the stare…

It got to Jonas, that stare. It said he was an idiot. It said Snowy did speak, you just had to know the language. It said you could let obstacles stand in your way, or you could find a way to move ahead. It said don't be a wimp, try a cookie.

Jonas didn't need a dog to tell him it was the same way with love. You could be an idiot or a coward. Or you could learn the language.

Jonas stared at the gingerbread, and then took a big bite.

~*~

Christmas Eve found Marnie lying beneath the stars once more.

In the distance, the lights of a plane descended on its approach to the airport. The sky was clear and velvety, blanketed with stars that waited humbly for lovers to appreciate them.

The day had been near perfect. She'd taken the Dreads and Alex to the zoo. In the late afternoon they'd returned to put the turkey in the oven, and then they'd driven through different neighborhoods, looking for something that was both charming (for Harriet) and safe (for Rodney). It would be nice to have family so close.

They'd set five places for dinner, including one for Jonas. He didn't show. Snowflake didn't run through the screen. And Marnie had to tell herself that was okay. It was just that she missed –

Snowflake appeared at her side, panting happily.

Marnie sat up and hugged him, whispering, "Don't leave without coming over for bacon in the morning." After tonight, there'd be no more slimed sessions, no more drool puddles, no more tackles. She should be happy.

"Merry Christmas." Jonas sat in the chair next to her, his face in shadow. "Handing out holiday hugs?"

Marnie had to stop herself from saying, "Yes." Instead, she said, "We missed you at dinner."

"I had to make the rounds to four different lots this evening, close them down, hand out paychecks and holiday bonuses, give some last minute advice so they'd stay out of trouble."

He'd said goodbye to his workers. And now he'd come to say goodbye to her. Marnie's heart panged.

"It's been great…And weird…" He couldn't seem to find the words. "The Dreads are one of a kind. You didn't actually believe Snowy could talk, did you?"

Marnie let out a frustrated noise that sounded a lot like something from Snowflake's repertoire. She wouldn't hurt the dog by denying she could understand him. She stroked the dog's velvety ears. "You're quiet tonight."

Snowflake panted without his usual gusto.

"He's been quiet all day," Jonas said. "He's depressed about having to leave."

Marnie didn't doubt the dog knew he was leaving in the morning.

"I'm depressed about leaving, too." The words were spoken in a soft rumble that Marnie might have attributed to Snowflake if the dog hadn't been practically in her arms.

She hugged the dog tighter.

"Do you know what I thought when I first saw you?" Jonas plucked her hands from Snowflake. "I thought you were okay."

"That's flattering." Not. She'd rather hear he found her beautiful or fascinating or irresistible.

"He sucks at this. Bail him out and kiss him." Snowflake rolled on his back and extended his gigantic paws in the air.

He doesn't want to kiss me, Marnie thought. *He's just saying a nice goodbye.*

"I…" Jonas stopped, as if he realized he sucked at this. "I thought: there's a woman who can take what life throws her and be okay."

"Oh."

"And then you told me about your past with this complete faith." He ran his thumbs over the back of her hands. "This faith that I'd understand where you'd been and what burdens you were carrying."

Marnie was hard pressed not to pull him close, to kiss whatever was bothering him and make it better.

"Somehow you knew I was a kindred spirit." He shook his head. "And I kept rejecting that connection, because you were right about things eating away at me, about me thinking I wasn't good or good enough." His voice hardened, grew distant. "I hit a car while chasing down a felon and killed the driver. I felt…I felt…100% responsible. As if I'd done something wrong, when it was the victim's fault. She pulled out without looking, without seeing, without knowing those were her last breathes."

Marnie couldn't breathe.

"No matter how many times I went over it, I couldn't find what I'd done wrong. I could only find myself to blame without any evidence to support it." His voice wavered. "People told me what I didn't want to believe. That it was an accident. That several things led up to the event, none of which were my fault. But…" His palm cupped her cheek. "It wasn't until you talked about the difference between feeling guilty and feeling like a bad person that I knew what they'd been trying to tell me. You led me to a different place inside of me, a more forgiving place. And for that I'll always be grateful."

But…There was a but coming. She could feel it.

Don't cry when he says goodbye.

"You're the kind of woman I'd always hoped to find – loves animals, great with kids, patient with stressed out cops and in-laws."

Don't cry. Don't cry.

"And you've got the strength to take on the difficulties life puts in your path." His hold on her hands tightened. "Rodney respects that you spoke up about his gun. I respect that you were able to come to a compromise. The Dreads really aren't all that dreadful."

Such beautiful words. She was going to cry. She only hoped she could hold on until after he walked away.

"Get to the point."

No. Marnie didn't want to hear his farewell.

"I'm a cop. I have to have my gun with me." The regret in his voice tore at her like an angry winter wind of the stormy coast. "But I hope you can respect that and find a compromise with me, because I think I'm falling in love with you," Jonas said, surprising her. "I hope you're falling in love with me. It would be the greatest Christmas present of all."

Marnie nearly fell off the lounger. But she didn't. She sat there and waited, because this couldn't be how her near disastrous Christmas turned into a perfect one. She had to be dreaming.

"Kiss already."

Marnie smiled. "Canine Cupid thinks you should kiss me."

"Yeah, I know. Smart dog," Jonas said, not that she believed he'd actually understood what Snowflake said. But who cared when he closed the distance between them and did as instructed?

There was nothing punishing or desperate about his kiss. It was tender and melancholy and accepting of himself, accepting of each other. Mostly, it was a promise of love.

Her hands twined through his thick hair as Jonas drew her closer, as she breathed him in, as she let her heart believe in love again.

And realized he tasted like gingerbread.

Epilogue

During a recent Skype session between Jonas and Darren, who'd called to check on Snowy...

I'm one lucky dog, dude.

When you go wheels up, I get to stay with your friends, who – let me tell you – may cook my kind of bacon, but are in a need of a lot of help in the love department.

I had an awesome Christmas with Jonas (did I mention bacon?), but he and Marnie's family ate most of my dog biscuits. Please come home and bake more soon.

Love, Snowy.

P.S. Maybe next time you'll let me stay with your friend Caroline. She seems lonely.

Thank you!

Thanks for reading Dog-Gone Christmas.

Sign up for my newsletter here: http://bit.ly/1hQOMIP and receive a free read, learn when my next book comes out or about contests I'm offering.

You can also follow me on Twitter at @MelCurtisAuthor or Facebook at www.facebook.com/MelindaCurtisAuthor

I write sweet romances for Harlequin, sweet romantic comedy novellas and have a limited backlist of sexier contemporary romances. I publish several books a year, so there's always something new coming out.

Brenda Novak says of Season of Change, *"Reading Slade and Christine's story reminded me of why I enjoy romance. Season of Change has found a place on my keeper shelf!"*

Jayne Ann Krentz says of Fool for Love, *"Sharp, sassy, modern version of a screwball comedy from Hollywood's Golden Age except a lot hotter."*

Dedication

I couldn't put words of love on the page without the love and support of my family, my book team, and my readers. Keep that good karma coming!

Bio

Melinda Curtis is an award-winning USA Today bestseller. She married her college sweetheart a long, long time ago. She writes sweet romance for Harlequin Heartwarming, sweet romantic comedy and sexy contemporary romances. They had three kids, who all moved away to go to college and never returned to their home state of California. Melinda and Mr. Curtis enjoy puttering around the house (okay, Melinda enjoys it more than her man), walking their Yorkie-Shih Tzu fur babies, and vacationing in sunny places. If you enjoy DIY and renovation shows, check out Melinda's Facebook page for some of their before and after pictures.

Made in the USA
Columbia, SC
20 June 2023